A SIMPLE KILL

NOLON KING

STERLING & STONE

Copyright © 2021 by Sterling & Stone

All rights reserved.

No part of this book may be reproduced in any form or by any electronic or mechanical means, including information storage and retrieval systems, without written permission from the author, except for the use of brief quotations in a book review.

The authors greatly appreciate you taking the time to read our work. Please consider leaving a review wherever you bought the book, or telling your friends about it, to help us spread the word.

Thank you for supporting our work.

Chapter One

Whoever said the pen is mightier than the sword never stared down the scope of a sniper rifle.

EMILY COULDN'T GET that thought out of her head. It was almost a curse, the way it kept cycling through her mind on repeat, working to make her feel better about the mountains of paperwork she had been asked to file. It wasn't the first time she'd imagined herself cresting a summit only to discover she was stuck on the ground floor of yet somewhere else she shouldn't be.

It had been a little over three months since she left the US Army and took a job with the FBI. Couldn't imagine her luck to land a spot in TOC — the Transnational Organized Crime division. RICO cases were notoriously difficult to prove and would be a worthy challenge to her.

Her first day had confirmed her suspicions — RICO cases were among the most complicated, and therefore the most rewarding. And she'd landed herself a big one. The white whale of organized crime. Despite arriving early, she'd barely had time to grab a cup of coffee before she was called into her first debriefing about the Outfit.

Now, just a scant quarter year since leaving the military for the Bureau, she was again immersed in a culture whose prime directive was to stop threats to her country and her people. And again, she was relegated to a support role. Non-essential. Non-relevant. Practically nonexistent.

It had been a hundred days since Simone's betrayal caused the festering emotional wound that was only now scarring over, and Emily feared more time behind the desk was going to rip it open again.

The army trained Emily for danger, but here she was serving her country by doing paperwork. She kept filing — in triplicate — losing days of her life cooped up in her boss's office, performing tasks that could be handled by just about anyone while her deadly skillset atrophied.

She looked up, caught yet another too-interested glance from the man himself — her boss, Deputy Director Henry Brasse — then quickly looked back down at her computer rather than attempting any more of his uncomfortable small talk. The office was small, and his awkward conversation brought it to the edge of claustrophobic.

The door burst open. Loud and sudden, unexpected enough to rattle just about anyone. Brasse jumped. Pretty sure he squeaked, just a little. But Emily barely flinched in her chair. She looked up to see Director Amanda Tepper striding into the office, flanked by a pair of men wearing funeral suits and indoor shades. Human echoes on either side of her, jaws as square as their flat-top haircuts.

Emily resisted the urge to salute as she rose. "Director."

Brasse fumbled to his feet after her. Mumbled a greeting that was impossible to understand. Looked more like a little boy about to get yelled at than a man in charge of the Bureau's largest RICO case.

"I'm going to need a moment with Wyatt." Tepper tipped her chin at Emily and awaited his response.

"Of course." But Brasse didn't go anywhere.

Tepper filled in the blanks for him. "I'll be needing your office."

"Yes, of course." His flustered face beaded with sweat. "Please, take your time."

He shuffled out of his office. After the door closed loudly behind him, Director Tepper's expression finally softened. She met Emily's gaze, the Men in Black still standing frozen behind her. "Please, sit."

Emily returned to her seat, heart pounding, wondering if she was in trouble ... *again*. Amanda Tepper never visited anyone without a good reason.

Her men stood by the door while she went to Brasse's desk, grabbed his chair, then dragged it across the office to sit near Emily. "Do you have any idea why I'm here?"

"No."

Tepper stared at her for too long, as if waiting for Emily to blink.

It was her turn to feel like a misbehaving child, but she didn't flinch.

Finally, the director said, "We have a job for you."

Again, Emily had to resist the urge to salute. "Of course. Whatever I can do."

Anything was better than filing paperwork in triplicate.

"You'll be going undercover to flush out the participants and host of a contest."

"A contest?" Everything about this felt weird. The air was unsettling. Not any warmer or colder, but somehow more electric. The men stood behind the director like angry idols.

"This is an unusual situation," Tepper acknowledged. "Contract killers will be given points for various kills."

"Points? Why? Is this some sort of training exercise?" She fired off the trio of questions like three pulls of the trigger.

"The winner will ultimately win a lucrative position in the Outfit."

"Oh." Now it made sense.

In the dozen weeks Emily had been with the FBI, she'd been working on this case. Which meant typing and filing countless reports. But Emily had read every note, every theory. Every word.

More importantly, she remembered all of it.

The Outfit appeared out of nowhere about a decade ago. A mob-like organization with seemingly unlimited funds and a compulsion to make all the rules. Or change them. They operated by way of chaos. The organization was still mostly a mystery, despite various government agencies having thrown money and manpower at the problem. And it was getting worse rather than better.

They'd been riling up law enforcement for a decade, but the general public still didn't know about them. The coverup was big but necessary. Even major media played ball the few times they'd been asked to. Fear was the Outfit's best weapon, and they were working to turn ignorant comfort into persistent terror in this country. From order to chaos, clarity to confusion, feast to famine. They wanted to see homes turn into hellscapes and companions into combatants.

The Outfit's best trick so far was in the trafficking of rumor and speculation. Little was known, less was shared. Emily hadn't had any idea the organization even existed until her reassignment.

"How does it work?" she asked. "What do you want me to do?"

Tepper was stone-faced. Bangs as straight as her chin.

"Whoever gets the most points first gets a meeting with the Foreman."

The Foreman — capo for the Outfit.

How had none of this crossed Emily's desk yet? And how much more did she not know?

"Points are kills, I assume."

The director nodded. "That's correct, but it's only the first level of the contest. The Foreman will reveal the final target to the winner. Once said target is eliminated, the killer will be awarded payment plus a position in the Outfit."

"I get the Outfit wants to eradicate rivals. What about the Bureau? Are we protecting these people, or do we also want them gone?" If it was the latter, it made sense that Tepper was asking her. With Emily's sniper training, she was the ideal candidate for the job. Or was she supposed to protect the targets?

One of her father's favorite sayings popped into her mind.

The enemy of my enemy is my friend. Unless he's my enemy, too.

Tepper frowned. "We don't know much about the contest, only that there is one. Right now, the targets are blind. Obviously, we'd want to protect those we can, either because they're law enforcement or because they're criminals who can turn state's evidence and help us build our case. In the end, I need you to get to the guy behind it all. Do whatever's necessary to get a face-to-face with the Foreman."

Whatever was necessary? Even if the target was law enforcement? That changed things.

"Wyatt, this is our best chance in a decade. If we can get the identities of both the Foreman and his ultimate target, we'll finally have everything we need to shut down the Outfit and also stop someone else from filling in the power vacuum left behind."

"You have the wrong person for this. I—"

"Save it, agent. You're exactly what we need in this situation."

"What about—"

"Your records will be made public," Tepper said. "With a few crucial edits."

"Crucial edits?"

"We created a new narrative for you. One that'll help you fit in undercover."

"I'm sorry?" Would have stung less if she'd been slapped across the face. This couldn't mean what she thought it did.

But of course, it did.

"Agent Wyatt, the Outfit will look into every contestant, and there is zero chance you could survive their scrutiny as-is. Or was. We needed to ruin your past to protect the present and secure our collective future. Do you understand?"

"I'm not sure I do," Emily admitted. But of course, she did. She just didn't want it to be true.

"We changed your bio. Gave you a bad conduct discharge."

A BCD? No. This couldn't be happening. She'd fought that action. And won, damn it. Her record was clean. Her discharge was honorable.

"We also created a social media profile that shows a former soldier who is highly disgruntled with the government. Made you a page on LiveLyfe dedicated to detailing personal and global injustices, plus a Fundid campaign to hint at some serious money issues. The Outfit can run all the psych profiles they want. What we've built will pass any and all of them."

"There must be somebody else."

"Multiple criteria make you an ideal candidate. You were cultivated for this long before now."

"Cultivated?"

"And you've come highly recommended."

"Bad conduct discharge ..." The words tasted bitter on her tongue.

Emily had completed Sniper School with the US Army before her honorable discharge had risen in the ranks to a classification of Military Occupational Specialty 11B, Infantry. Serving her country was exactly where she had always wanted to be. Emily had idolized her father — an Army Ranger and unparalleled sniper. Then he died protecting his country. She was only ten at the time and had never stopped grieving. There wasn't even a body to mourn or say goodbye to. Her father was just *gone*.

It was at that empty-casket funeral when Emily vowed to *be all she could be* to honor him.

Despite the conflict it caused with her mom — getting over the loss of her husband was agonizing enough, she couldn't stand the thought of losing her daughter, too — Emily spent her life in worship of that promise.

She was an overachiever, but sometimes gender worked against her. She wasn't accepted into Sniper School until her third request then flunked out due to sabotage. Took a lot of time and effort to prove it had happened, more time and effort to fight the bad conduct discharge. When her name was finally cleared and she'd been reinstated, she'd had to wait several more weeks for the next training session to begin.

Even though Emily ultimately graduated at the top of her class, she was still frozen out. Because of the cloud surrounding the sabotage? Because she was a woman? A combination of both? It was hard to say. But she hadn't been chosen to liaise with any of the Ranger groups, nor had she been given any individual missions. Found herself riding a desk, instead, marking time until her *honorable* discharge. All that, just to wind up riding another desk with the FBI's TOC Division and waiting for Brasse to trust her with something more substantial than filling out forms.

With no other choice, she reported for duty every day, left her complaints unvoiced, and told herself her sniper skills would be put to better use someday. All the while knowing it was highly unlikely.

Now Emily was getting that chance, by way of making the bad conduct discharge look like the end of her military story. Sabotage all over again.

"I'm sorry." Despite the severity of Tepper's expression, she seemed sincere. "It isn't fair, but it's the only way. According to your new records, several altercations with a superior earned your eventual discharge."

Of course, she'd had altercations. She'd been *sabotaged* by her superior. But Emily had been vindicated and the BCD had been reversed. This was so unfair!

"That dismissal led to some understandable anti-government sentiment on your part that grew increasingly corrosive over time. We're working with LiveLyfe to backdate the page. All the way back to your original hearing."

That was nearly two years ago!

"Filling it with a lot of political ranting and a growing desperation. We have a writer working to mimic your voice and an AI sweep that's reading at a ninety-four percent match. You made your last post two weeks ago. You're totally broke and very angry."

"Two weeks ago?" Emily kept the anger out of her voice, but that only boiled her insides. "You mean this is already live?"

Tepper's companions bristled at Emily's rising ire — barely a twitch, but she saw it.

"Nothing's live yet," Tepper said. "But it will be. You don't have to worry about this being everywhere. Your regular profiles still exist. These are in addition to rather than instead of. We can't change history or what people already know about you. Too obvious, too many red flags. But it works to our favor to create a side profile for you. It will look like you were trying to keep this part of your life hidden. The real you will look like a cover to the Outfit."

"Will my mom be able to see it?" Emily knew the answer, but she blurted the question anyway.

"It's public, so your mother could theoretically see it, yes. But she would have to be looking."

"Can I tell her the truth? If she asks?"

"No, you may not."

She wasn't comfortable with the character smear and hated that her mother might read them, as she would then believe the lies. But that was a temporary situation. Emily would be honored to serve her country and help to topple the Outfit. Maybe even be a hero like her father.

Emily looked into Tepper's eyes. There was still something the director wasn't telling her.

"Why me? There's something else, besides my scores or—"

"I told you we've been planning this for a long time."

Ah. The key word Emily had overlooked before. "We?"

Tepper gave an uncharacteristic pause before replying. "You were recommended by Simone Bisset. The two of you will be working together."

Her heart fell to her feet. "No." Emily shook her head. "No. I'm sorry, but no. I can't work with her. No."

She would work with anyone else. Anyone at all. But Simone Bisset? The bitch had sabotaged her in Sniper

School and permanently soiled her chance for a spotless record. Sure, the BCD had been reversed, but the stigma remained. Emily had never been happier than when she left the military for the Bureau and knew she'd never have to see the woman again.

But now they were in the same company, apparently working the same case. And now Simone was doing it again. The social media smear campaign and BCD were probably both her ideas.

"Simone says you're perfect for the job, and from everything I've seen, I agree."

"I don't trust her!"

Emily was a bit too loud. Again, the men flinched forward.

Tepper stood without responding, dragged her chair back over to Brasse's desk, then started to approach the door. Both men turned in formation.

Emily jumped to her feet. "Wait!"

Tepper turned back, expectant but silent.

The men also turned, silent but tensed.

If working with her former nemesis was the best way for Emily to serve her country, then of course she would do it. "How long do I have to decide?"

"There is no mission without trust." Tepper stared at her. "Can you trust Simone Bisset?"

It didn't matter who Simone was working for, Emily could never trust her. Not after what she did.

"I can trust her," she lied.

Tepper nodded, still looking at Emily, the men once more like statues beside her. "Then the answer is now."

"I'm sorry?"

"That's how long you have to decide."

"Can I meet with Simone first?"

"You can meet the moment you agree to the mission," Tepper told her.

Emily drew a deep breath. Held it for a pregnant second. Exhaled through pursed lips, a slow and silent vent that did nothing to clear the air. "It would be my honor to accept this mission and serve my country."

She could only hope she wasn't making the biggest mistake of her life.

Chapter Two

EMILY HAD NOT ONLY REQUESTED an audience with Simone, she'd asked if they could meet in private, never expecting Tepper to agree. Especially considering their earlier exchange about trust.

But the Director had nodded. "You have one hour."

"I won't need that long. I just need to get a few things straight."

"The hour is at the request of Bisset. Now, come with me."

They walked in silence for about five minutes, then Tepper paused outside a small shack. "See you on the other side."

Emily had about a million questions she wanted to ask, but she wasn't given a chance. Tepper stepped to the side while one of her two chaperones opened the door, waited for Emily to enter the shack, then closed the door behind her.

There was one other person in the room — Simone Bisset.

"It's good to see you, Emily," Simone said. "We don't have much time, so let's go ahead and get started."

But Emily ignored her.

Then they stared at one another for a while — a long while — in frosty silence, each waiting to see who would flinch from the standoff first.

Simone grunted. At her, about her ... Emily wasn't sure. Nor did she care.

No one spoke. The secondhand ticking was the only sound in the room.

The snake opened a folder on the table in front of her, scribbled something on a paper inside it, closed the file, then stared at Emily again.

Probably an attempt at intimidation.

Didn't work.

They'd been given an hour. One quarter was gone and still no words.

The clock continued to tick.

Emily was tempted to break the silence. She had called the meeting, after all. It irked her that Simone requested an hour, so Emily wanted to eat into it as much as she could. Her point had been proven already. Now she was just being stubborn. But even though she knew it, Emily couldn't stop herself.

For another five minutes, she stared.

Simone finally sighed, and Emily readied herself to answer whatever question left her former mentor's mouth. But then Simone returned to her regularly scheduled breathing and left Emily wondering what was next.

Another five minutes passed.

The next deep sigh belonged to Emily. Still, neither woman spoke.

Less than a minute later, Simone finally broke the silence. "I'm only trying to help you."

Emily sneered, both delighted with her minor victory and disgusted with Simone's pathetic — and obviously untrue — ice breaker. "I remember the last time you tried to help me."

"That wasn't what you—"

"Let me guess ... I'm supposed to feel bad for you, right? This is where you unload your pitiable sob story? Save the spiel, I've already heard it."

"Emily—"

"You grew up dirt poor, and your grades weren't good enough for scholarships."

"This isn't—"

"Not because you weren't smart but because you worked two jobs after school, and that kept you away from your homework. The military was the only way you could get into college, right?" Emily leaned forward, narrowing her eyes at Simone. "'We're different, but the same.' That's what you said to me. If not the day we met, then goddamn close."

Simone stared back at Emily, no longer interrupting.

"My father had to die before I was interested in joining, but thanks to your deadbeat mom and absentee daddy, you were willing to enlist the minute you legally could. You're competitive and guarded. You never let people get to know the real you since you see yourself as inherently unlovable. At least, you did until you joined up and finally found yourself. Now you're 'Army Strong,' right? It's your mission in life to help girls like me, even though you're not much older. Let me know if I got anything wrong."

"You were always spot on with the details."

"These were especially easy. I wrote what you said in my journal. Sometimes I read those old entries when I want to remind myself how shitty humans can be."

"We're running out of time."

"We have this room for an hour. At your request, remember?"

"I had to allow for your wasting fifteen minutes."

"Don't act like you knew that would happen," Emily said. Almost spat.

Simone turned the folder, so it faced Emily, nudged it forward, then gestured for her to open it.

Emily hesitated, but then she reached out, flipped over the cover, and saw what Simone had written.

18 minutes.

She closed the folder then shoved it back across the table. "I'm glad you know me so well." A beat later, she said, "How the hell am I supposed to trust you?"

"Take a leap of faith. You can kill me if I cross you."

"Can I kill you if you don't?" Emily asked.

"What happened between us will never happen again. You have my word."

"Your word is irrelevant."

"I had my reasons, even if you think they were wrong."

"Even if *I think* they were wrong?"

"I'm not a malicious person, Emily. But, as you so eloquently put it, my life was once a pitiable sob story. I could have wallowed in my misfortune. Raged at the world and done nothing to better my station. Instead of becoming a burden to society and a bitter old lady, I chose to help myself. The Army was my out. Then, somewhere along the way, it became less about my survival and more about the mission. I was serving our country. Making the world a better, safer place. And my life was better for it, too. So, I decided not to let anyone hold me back or derail my ambitions. In the military, that meant I obeyed every command without hesitation in my pursuit of advancement, and I eventually landed the job I wanted because of it. Never once did I question the sabotage I was ordered to carry out."

"Ordered to carry out? You did that to me two years ago. You left the Army six months after that. I don't know when you started working for the Bureau, or even how you passed the security clearance with a BCD on your record, but you couldn't have been here when you tried to ruin me."

"I've been with the Bureau for three years, Emily. My big chicken dinner is as fake as yours. And finding you was my first assignment. What I did to you? All part of the job."

Emily's head spun. All this time, all this pain … and none of it was real?

Then she shook her head, crossed her arms. Glared at the chameleon seated across from her. "Nice try. Could have won an Oscar for that performance. I don't know how you ended up here, but I do know you're twisting everything, so you look like the good guy in all this. You can't fool me. Never again. It was me you tried to ruin. *Me.* I thought we were friends. Or at least building a rapport."

"We were. You were the only person I could even remotely relate to. That's one of the reasons I chose you."

"If that's what you think a friend is, I hate to see how you treat your enemies."

"You take this job, and you see it first-hand." Her voice was cold. Her eyes, colder.

Again, Emily paused and considered what Simone was saying. Then again, she steeled herself and refused to buy into the lie. "I'm not going to let you change the subject. And I'm certainly not going to let you play the victim. You did this to me."

"That's true. I did. I've admitted so."

"And now you're trying to screw me again!"

Simone shook her head. "We don't have all day for you to figure this out. I'm not the bad guy. Everything I did, no matter how painful you found it, was to establish your cover."

"Bullshit. You have people working on my cover now. What you did was competitive and selfish and evil."

"Emily, I can't change the past. But you're not stupid. You know an electronic cover only goes so far. We needed witnesses to your cheating and your BCD. We needed you to believe it was happening so everyone around you would believe it, too."

"But everyone knows I got it reversed. You were the one dining on the big chicken dinner. Wish you had choked on it."

Simone sighed. "That was my fault. We were trying to keep the circle small, but we should have read in Command. But we didn't know if the Outfit had any moles in your unit, and this op is big. We couldn't take the chance of blowing our cover. I read you wrong. I didn't think you'd fight the charge. Definitely didn't think you'd win when it was a he-said/she-said against your superior officer."

"You aren't my superior anything."

"You need to grow up, Emily. This is bigger than you and me."

"You said you wanted to mentor me."

"I did," Simone insisted.

"So that I would trust you."

"Yes, but also because I had a fucking job to do." Simone dropped all pretense of civility. Her tone dripped with venom, and she reared back in her seat, a viper poised to strike.

At least she was finally showing her true colors.

"You say I have the sob story? What about your pity

party, Emily? You've done nothing but rant and rave over what I did to you, even though I was following orders. Yeah, you fought for your name, which actually made my job harder, but what have you done for yourself since then? You never fought for a spot on a Ranger team. And wasn't that your goal?"

Emily's gut burned. Her face flamed. Her rage ignited. "How dare you? You have no idea how difficult it is to land a spot on one of the teams. Especially for a woman! I did fight, until I realized you'd tarnished my reputation too much for anyone to take a chance on me."

"Yeah. It was my fault."

"It was! But I kept fighting. I chose to work for the FBI. I applied and got the job I wanted. I did that. My work. My sweat. My sacrifice. That's how I got where I am. And I didn't need to spin a web of lies to do it."

"You think your merit is how you landed a position in a coveted department on the most important RICO case we have? Didn't you find the application process a bit on the easy side? The scrutiny a tad lax? The interviews smooth and comfortable not very intense?"

The prospect stole her breath. Her heart rate spiked, the pounding painful in her chest. "No. I won't let you do this again. You can't take that from me, too. I *earned* my spot in the Bureau."

"Wrong again, Emily. I fucking gift-wrapped it for you. You might not like my methods, but regardless of what happened, you can never say I haven't been there for you. I helped you plenty. You just didn't know it."

If it was true — and Emily had a sick feeling it might be, at least to some extent — then she might not be qualified for the work she was doing. Rather than admit her concerns, she doubled down on her accusations. "Assuming what you say is true, and I think we both know it's not, you only helped me because it was in your best interests. You say you were only following orders? Whose? Tepper's? She'd never have done this."

"We — the Bureau — have been working on moving you into position for a while now. The circle was kept small, but it wasn't one person calling the shots. Even this whole department doesn't know your true history. That information is given out only on a need-to-know basis. Most of this group doesn't need to know. And, until now, you didn't, either."

That explained so much. Months of working here, and most of the department kept her at arm's length. Not because she was bad at her job or an inherently unlikable person. Not because Brasse kept her confined to his office and only on administrative tasks. No, it was because she'd been labeled a liability before she'd started. She wanted to snarl but managed to keep it inside. "I'm glad you finally decided to read me in."

"You know how this works, Emily. You can't take it personally."

"I think I can. You used me, destroyed me, then left me all alone."

"I knew it would only be temporary," Simone said.

"Bullshit. You didn't care at all."

"I did care. It ruined me to see how devastated you were at getting booted out of the program. After the training I'd been through, I didn't even think it was possible for me to feel guilt anymore. But it hit me like hellfire afterward. I've apologized, but I'll do it again since you still don't believe me. I really am sorry."

Emily flared her nostrils. "I'll never believe you."

"Then tell me what to do. How am I supposed to fix this?" Simone sat straighter in her chair. "We may never be friends. I can understand and accept that. But it's in our best interest to have a strong working relationship. One where we can be cordial and have to trust and respect each other. How do you propose we get to that point? Because it is necessary, Emily. And not just for your peace of mind, but for the good of the world."

Emily had never seen her more sober. And for the first time since the silent standoff at the beginning of the meeting, she didn't know what to say.

Simone sighed. "I get it. You hate me and don't how or if you can ever trust me again. Assuming time does heal all our wounds, we don't have enough of it. So, we need to build a bridge, even if it's a temporary one. Because right now, we're a team, whether you like it or not. And if we can't trust each other, we'll both end up dead."

Too many thoughts tumbled through her head. Too many emotions spiraled out of control. "I was wrong. I never should have accepted this assignment. I want out."

"And what will you tell Tepper? You already agreed to the mission."

"Why don't I tell her you have no honor? She seems like someone who will give a shit about that."

"I have plenty of honor, Emily."

"That's what you said the last time, before you manipulated and betrayed me."

"That's because your definition of honor is bullshit. What matters is *doing the right thing*. We're in an ugly business, and sometimes our job forces us to do ugly things. You became a sniper, for God's sake. You are trained to kill people for a living. But you take exception when someone else might need to lie or cheat or steal in order to finish the mission?"

"A kill order is for the good of the country. But the immorality you traffic in? You're hurting your own people." Emily shook her head. "I think there's a big difference between manipulating an enemy to stop them from doing something evil and doing the same thing to a sister-in-arms and supposed friend."

"I understand that's the story you need to tell yourself. To stroke your ego, stave off the guilt, or get a good night's sleep, but—"

"Why am I really here?"

"You know why you're here. I recommended you because I believe in you, and that meant I needed to get you kicked out of the military, thereby blackballing you from respectable circles."

"You mean rip my dream away from me."

"To give you a better one," Simone said.

"You have no idea what I want."

"I know *exactly* what you want." Then she stared, daring Emily to challenge her.

"What I *want* is to trust the people I'm working with, and that isn't you. The last time I handed you my faith, it was repaid with betrayal."

"That will never happen again," Simone said, her eyes wide and glassy.

"Convincing. Just like the last time."

And then they were back to staring. Until Simone finally stood with a sigh. "I can't believe I'm saying it again, but I am. I'm sorry. But this time, it's for a different reason. I was wrong to do what I did, but only because I was wrong about you."

"What's that supposed to mean?"

"I've made a mistake. The Army, Sniper School, the BCD? Those things should have rinsed the melodrama right out of you, but you're clearly still too emotional, and therefore ill-equipped, to handle this mission."

"You lied to me."

"I did my job," Simone spat. "Do you want to do yours?"

She swallowed. "Are we supposed to be working together? Or am I just taking orders from you?"

"Because your cover is a bad conduct discharge, there can't be any record of you talking to government personnel. You'll be cut off from all official channels. I also have a cover, and I'll be your only contact."

"If you have a tarnished record, too, how are you able to talk to Brasse or Tepper or anyone else?"

"Last chance, Emily. Are you in or are you out? I won't ask again."

She stood toe to toe with Simone and looked her directly in her eyes. "I'm going to do this because I'm a better sniper, a better American, and a better person than you."

"Your reasons are your reasons." She held Emily's gaze.

"I'll kill you if you double cross me again."

"I know." Simone nodded, extending her hand for Emily.

They shook, neither breaking eye contact.

"So, what's next?" Emily asked.

"Say goodbye to everyone you know." Her face was stone-cold sober, her tone even more so.

She was only trying to scare Emily. Still, it bore repeating, a mantra in her mind.

Say goodbye to everyone you know.

"It starts now." A beat after that bombshell, she dropped another. "You have half an hour to handle any personal business. After that, we head to a hotel and begin to live our cover story."

Life, as Emily knew it, was officially over. No point putting it off any longer.

"I don't need to call anyone."

"No one?" Simone challenged her.

It wasn't enough to say she was better than Simone — in every way. Emily would prove it at every opportunity. "No one," she repeated.

Simone nodded then led Emily to another shack.

This one needed Simone's thumbprint to enter. It was empty except for an elevator that descended for what felt like a dozen floors, maybe more. Emily couldn't know for sure since there weren't any buttons inside the car, and she wasn't about to ask Simone anything about … well, anything.

Before the doors whispered open, Emily regretted not calling her mom. But she just had no idea what kind of bullshit she would have to manufacture on the fly and wasn't about to wing it in front of Simone. Her old mentor was her shadow for now, but Emily would eventually ditch her. Then, she'd call her mother. It would give her time to think of a strong cover.

The cavernous room wasn't at all what Emily expected. It didn't look like a war room, not that she'd ever seen one outside of the movies. There were no banks of computers, no wall-sized screens displaying maps of targets. It looked like an office. Just a horde of whiteboards, filing cabinets, and desks occupied by no more than two dozen people.

"What is this place?"

"It's everything we know about the Outfit."

"I've been working on the Outfit for months. Brasse doesn't have half of this intel."

"I know."

Emily cocked an eyebrow.

"Follow me." Simone led her around to a desk at the rear of the cluster without introducing Emily to anyone.

Benefit of the doubt? Maybe she didn't want to interfere with their work. Everyone seemed fixed on something.

More likely she was trying to keep Emily on the outside while cementing her position within.

Simone sat in an old, worn office chair and gestured for Emily to take the seat across from her. "You're probably wondering why we're here. And why your office doesn't know about this place."

"You have a leak," Emily guessed.

"This hangar is offline and off the record. Much of what we know about the Outfit, we've kept to ourselves. And a lot of the bullshit they want us to believe, we've circulated. That way, they think their misinformation campaign is working. This is where we keep the truths we're at least reasonably sure they don't know we know."

"Reasonably sure?"

"It's the Outfit." Simone shrugged. "We can't be sure about anything."

"I'm sure you're sure of something."

"We're sure the organization is dangerous," Simone said. "Brutal but intelligent. Have spies in Fortune 500 firms and in mom-and-pop shops. And in the government. They're careful. Not nearly as crazy as they need us to believe."

"Why *need* and not *want*?" Emily asked.

"Someone is directing all of this. Nothing's done on a whim. Every step has been calculated, prepared for."

"By the Foreman?"

Simone tucked a long strand of hair behind her ear. "If there really is such a person."

"You don't think the Outfit really has a capo?"

"We don't know if there is or isn't one. There could be a whole boardroom full of geniuses calling the shots, making the whole idea of the Foreman another ruse."

"What do *you* think?" Emily asked, more hooked than she wanted to be. She never should have started with, *what is this place?*

Simone pulled a deck of cards from a desk drawer. She flicked it open with her thumb, spilled them face up onto her desktop, then looked down at them. "Do you see all the kings?"

"Did you have that deck of cards in your drawer just waiting for this moment?" Emily leaned forward, craning her head toward the drawer. "What else do you have in there?"

"Do you see them or not?"

Emily looked down at Simone's desk. "Of course, I see them."

"Do you see the queens and jacks?"

Another glance. "Yes."

"How about the joker?"

"I see all the cards," Emily said. "And I'm sure you have a point, so can we hurry up and get there?

Simone swept her hand across the cards and shuffled them around on her desk. "How about now?"

"What?" Emily asked.

"Or now?" Simone rearranged the cards with another sweep.

"I don't—"

"I think the Foreman is a moving target because there isn't only one person. I subscribe to the boardroom theory. There are several people in charge, directing activities by majority. And they probably have enough support staff to constantly reconfigure reality." Simone jabbed her finger atop one of the kings and held it there. "The Foreman, be it a single person or a collective entity, wants us looking here, when we should really be looking *here*." She moved her finger from the king to a joker, half-buried under the edge of an ace.

"I appreciate the theater, but I'm not really sure what I'm supposed to be getting from this. Are you making a point and you're just not very good at it?"

Simone gave her a thin-lipped smile. "I'm trying to illustrate the danger—"

"I'm not a child. You shanghaied me into this operation, so talk to me straight."

"The Outfit is an operation, not a thing. Unlike the mafia, this isn't a clan where members pledge their lifelong loyalty. This is something different. The mafia used to be about ancestry, heritage, and old-world connections, family ties and blind obedience … this is something we don't understand yet."

"What's the biggest difference?"

"Money."

Not much difference there. "As in, the Outfit has more or less?"

"As in, we have no idea. Not about any of it. We know where the mob's money comes from, and we can trace a lot of history. The mafia got most of its power a century ago. Like any smart business, they knew when it was time to diversify. They went from alcohol, gambling, and prostitution to human trafficking, illegal drugs, and assassination for hire. Families started moving their money to legitimate investments as well."

"Right," Emily said. "We know this story. A government of checks and balances — the mob made out checks and politicians improved their balances."

"For a long time. But RICO made that harder, and this is something new."

"How new? When did we first encounter the Outfit?"

Simone shrugged. "Hard to know, we—"

"When did we first hear the word associated with the organization?"

"It's been about a decade, but things didn't start really heating up until a couple of years ago. Now the situation is getting out of control, and we need to keep a lid on this thing before it blows up and throws the entire country into a panic."

"Why would they panic?" Emily asked. "It's not like America is terrified of the mob."

"Because fear is the Outfit's currency. And it's only a matter of time before they have the entire country spending it. This entire situation is a ticking clock."

"You must have a theory on where this all started. What is it?"

"Say, you're in the mob and you want to get out. What are your options?"

"Death, prison, or state's evidence," Emily answered.

"Exactly. We have more than a few people on the books who supposedly left organized crime with the full sponsorship of the United States Government."

"You think the Outfit was started by someone in the Witness Protection Program?"

"Or several someones," Simone said.

That was interesting, and a twist Emily hadn't expected. The thrill of a mission was already alive in her blood. She pictured herself peering through her scope, waiting for the perfect shot. Squeezing the trigger, eliminating her target. One shot later, the world would be a slightly better place.

But that would only happen if she could trust Simone, and right now the jury was still very much out on whether Emily could ever do that again. Everything seemed fine right now. Simone appeared sincere.

Appeared.

Same as the first time she'd tried to destroy Emily's life.

It would be easy to get sucked in again. Fall for the same traps, make the same mistakes. End up back on the bottom.

We had to create your bad conduct discharge backstory.

Maybe Simone was telling the truth and betrayal had been part of the plan all along. Proof of her deception had come easily, and the hearing reversing the original charge had gone notoriously well. Maybe too smoothly. Could have all been a set-up to establish her cover while not leaving her high and dry afterward.

Or she'd had the proper evidence to clear her name and prove Simone was the guilty party.

She sighed. It was impossible to know for certain. And as Simone was the only one she could discuss the issue with, she had no impartial source to help her see the situation clearly.

Still, conversation came easier after that. Emily didn't stop asking questions, and though Simone was an exceptional liar, the speed and depth at which she answered every query once they got going was impressive enough. If she had alternate responses prepared, then she was impressively duplicitous, considering Emily took a hard left whenever she could. But if Simone was making up her replies on the fly while somehow accounting for her answers and keeping them all straight, then she had an extraordinary, almost impossible level of control and should work for the CIA, not the FBI.

Emily would have to remain vigilant, constantly on alert, aware of the slightest inconsistency.

And ready to kill Simone the second it became clear it was necessary.

"You look exhausted," Simone said after three hours of talking.

"I'm not tired at all." But Emily had bitten her bottom lip a few minutes ago to stifle a yawn. Drew blood and still almost lost the battle.

"Let's get some air."

"If you want to," Emily said.

Simone gave her a knowing smile as she stood. This time, on the way out, she introduced her to a few people — Abraham, Noom, Flora, and Jack. They seemed fierce. And glad to have another hand at the Outfit's throat.

Emily was starting to trust Simone despite herself, but that only made her more suspicious.

"How are you doing?" Simone asked as they entered the elevator.

"Are you asking if I feel capable of doing my job or if I've forgiven you?"

"I'm asking how *you* are doing. It's been a long day, and I'm sure your head is full. There's baggage between us. And you didn't take the time to properly say your goodbyes when you had the chance. That's probably weighing on you now."

"You don't know what is or isn't weighing on me," Emily said, even though of course it was like carrying a hundred-pound sack of rocks.

Simone didn't respond.

A *ding* announced they'd reached their destination. The elevator doors opened.

They walked through the empty shack then stepped outside. Emily's foot wasn't even on the ground before her phone sounded like a pinball game. She pulled it from her pocket then looked at the lock screen. Seven missed calls and twenty-six texts — an even dozen from her mother.

Her pulse started pounding.

"Do you need to make a call?" Simone asked.

Her heart still a hammer at her ribcage, Emily felt surprisingly submissive. "May I?"

"Five minutes. Then I'll need to take your phone."

Emily was already dialing. Mom picked up on the first ring.

"Is it true?" she said instead of *hello*.

"Is what true?" Emily turned around and glared at Simone. *What did you do?*

Simone stared back, her expression and body both frozen.

"I thought the dishonorable discharge—"

"Not dishonorable, Mom. Bad conduct discharge."

"What's the difference?"

"Dishonorable discharges are much worse."

"Well, 'bad conduct' doesn't exactly sound good!"

She wasn't wrong. "I know. But—"

"You said the ruling was reversed. You said—"

"Where did you hear about the discharge?"

"So, it is true?"

"Where did you hear it, Mom?"

"You know I read your LiveLyfe. And even if I didn't, Mary does, and she—"

"What did I say on the post?" Emily asked.

Simone's eyes were suddenly fierce, and her stare turned harder. *Be careful.*

"You don't remember?" Mom asked.

"I was really drunk," Emily lied.

"At ten in the morning?"

This was exactly why she'd wanted time to plan, and no audience, when she talked to her mother. "I've been having a really rough time."

Emily loathed the lie as she spoke it.

"Oh, dear. Why didn't you say something? I could have—"

"This is something I have to deal with on my own." Her voice had gone from frantic to flat.

Mom had been trying not to cry, the tremor in her voice had made that obvious. Now, she lost the ability to hold her tears. They came in heavy, heaving sobs. Each of them another icepick stab into Emily's heart.

"I'm sorry, Mom. I don't know what to say." She really didn't.

"After your father's sacrifice … he would be so disappointed in you."

Mom sounded as pained as Emily felt.

She wanted to insist on her innocence, but there were just too many reasons she couldn't. Instead, Emily tried to apologize again. Tried and failed. The words stuck in her throat, refused to leave. Mom was right. Her father was an honorable man. This would have destroyed him.

Emily could hear his voice in her head.

Stand for right, Emily. Even if it means standing alone. The honorable are always accountable to their own code of conduct.

"I know, Mom," Emily said, voice breaking. After a shuddering breath, she added, "I love you." Then she ended the call.

"Are you okay?" Simone asked.

"I'm fine."

She held out her hand, waiting for Emily's phone.

"Why did you let me keep it in the first place if you were only going to take it?"

"Because you didn't talk to your mom before our briefing, and I knew you would need to."

"You said the stuff on social media wouldn't be obvious. You lied to me. Again."

"Apparently they made a different decision. I had nothing to do with that." No apology, only another cold stare from Simone. "Are you ready to do this or not?"

"Can I have a moment to process that my life has just been ruined?"

"Stop being so weak," Simone said. "This is just getting started. Most people who go undercover surrender their IDs, too. Be glad you still get to be you."

Yeah, because that was such a picnic at the moment.

"I know your homelife was less than ideal, Simone, but it isn't weak to love your mother. Or to care about what she thinks of you."

"No, it isn't. Your feelings are natural. But it is debilitating to let them hold you back."

"Family and honor matter more than anything else. You just wouldn't know that because no one could ever love or trust a born liar like you."

"Family and honor are luxuries for those who can afford them." Simone held her hand out, more insistent. "Now give me your phone and grow the hell up."

Emily surrendered her phone while making raw meat of her bottom lip.

Fine. Whatever. She was still the best asset here.

"What now?" Emily asked.

"Follow me."

Chapter Three

EMILY DIDN'T WANT to suspect Simone, but she couldn't quell her misgivings or screaming intuition.

There was something cold about her that Emily hadn't seen before, back when she was still enamored with the woman. Charmed by her insincerity, clueless she'd been living her life as a puppet on a string throughout their short relationship.

Now, Simone couldn't say anything right. If she was pragmatic or icy, Emily saw it as evidence of her disconnection and a likely indicator of a set-up. And if Simone was kind, Emily couldn't help but take that déjà vu as proof that she was about to pull something shady.

They were back underground. At Simone's desk, which was covered with piles of files. It had to be dark up top by now. It had been a long day, and Emily was feeling vacant. Emptier than exhausted, though she would never admit it to Simone. She was losing her focus, which was probably exactly what her handler wanted.

"How about him?" Simone pointed to photo.

"Garfield." Then, before Simone could move to the next two right beside it, she said, "Arcade and Cosmo."

"Excellent." She produced another photo from a separate file. A woman with very straight, very blonde hair. "How about her?"

"Jackie-O. One of three female assassins known to have accepted at least one assignment from the Outfit."

Simone smiled. "Great job."

Emily didn't want the flattery to feel good, so she told herself it didn't. Same as she ignored the shiver of tender affection that rippled through her, certain it was only a stain from where Simone had infiltrated her psyche the last time. Emily hadn't wanted to let her in then, either, but even if Simone was only a few years older, she was still the closest thing to a father figure Emily had known since she lost her dad to a terminal case of valor.

It was a balm to her uncertainty to have someone looking out for her like that. To be taking such an active interest in her future. Simone had been where Emily was not all that long ago, so why not mentor her? Slowly gain her trust before the betrayal.

At first, Emily blamed herself. But there was no way she could have seen it coming. Simone had been a little too good at her job. Emily believed she cared until her face was shoved in the truth.

And that's what made the Simone sitting across from her now so impossible to trust.

She oscillated between opposites. Warm one minute, icy the next. Simone acknowledged what had happened but was in no way contrite. Sure, she'd apologized. But it didn't seem sincere. Especially since she immediately justified her actions, anyway. A necessary deception, Simone insisted every time. There was no other way to get Emily to where she was now, and this was exactly where she was supposed to be.

In other words, Simone was still following orders, this time by following the script and solemnly swearing to never betray Emily again.

It all seemed a little too gift wrapped, and Emily couldn't trust it at all.

For now, the best she could do was to pay close attention to every single thing Simone was doing.

"How about this one?"

Emily looked down at the photo. *Lucy.* A man, with bright red hair the length and style of vintage Lucille Ball. She wondered if maybe someone had once commented on the assassin's hair, then he went with it. In name and everything else.

"That's Lucy," Emily answered.

"And if you see him?"

"He's a priority one target."

"Exactly." Simone smiled.

And there it was again.

Emily just couldn't trust her, couldn't shake feeling like Simone was setting her up for something on the field. What if getting Emily to shoot Lucy was the real plan all along? Throw her under the bus for not following orders to bring him in alive.

Worse, what if Simone was a mole for the Outfit? If Emily followed her orders, she could very well be doing exactly what the Foreman wanted.

She needed time to process.

"Mind if I recap what we have so far?"

"Please." Simone gestured down at the pile of everything.

Emily waved her hand loosely in the air, indicating the

desks, whiteboards, and filing cabinets. "This is everything not online that we know about the Outfit, right?"

"That's correct."

"And out of the hundreds of people investigating the Outfit, or I guess probably thousands by now, the handful of us here in the Batcave are the only ones off-book. Yes?"

Now clearly curious, Simone said, "We report to Tepper, but otherwise, that's right."

Emily gestured at Simone's desktop. "So, to summarize, this is your curated information from the cream of everything we have, hand-selected to help us. And when it's added all together, we still know less than dick."

"We know a lot."

"Most of today has been filled with all the things we don't know!" Emily exclaimed.

A few people glanced over, but most of the room ignored her, and even those who had looked barely flinched before turning back.

In a level voice, Simone said, "We know the Outfit showed up as a dangerous wildcard. We know they wanted a certain kind of attention, so we starved them of oxygen. We know something big is happening, and this contest is in the middle of whatever that something is. So, we need to be, too. And we know if we fail, that's probably it. The country will know there's a chaotic cell within our borders, one we cannot control."

"Couldn't the Outfit prove that now if they wanted to?"

"They could."

"So, why haven't they?"

"They've been waiting for something."

Simone's face had gone sallow, but Emily didn't need to see it. She finally realized the gravity of the situation and was now feeling it chew through her skin.

"And this is that something." It wasn't a question.

"We think so." Simone gave an almost imperceptible nod.

Emily sat up straighter. "Why did you wait so long to bring me in?"

"We found out about the contest yesterday."

"But you set me up—"

"We were preparing. Something like this was inevitable, we just didn't know when. And I always knew you were the right person for this."

"What is *this*?" Emily asked.

"Our chance.

"What makes us special?"

"The Outfit has eyes everywhere, but our identities have been crafted to fit this scenario from the start."

"My identity wasn't crafted, Simone. I am who I am. As for you …" She shrugged and let that comment dangle there.

Simone didn't take the bait. "Our *covers* have been crafted to fit this situation. I chose you as soon as I saw you, Emily. Someday you'll understand why I did what I did and stop being so mad about it. Maybe the day before you thank me. For now, know this — you were reassigned to this RICO case for a reason. The Bureau needed you familiar with the Outfit well before the inevitable mission. Today was about teaching you how to think about what you already knew."

"It's great that you're teaching me how to think about stuff I already know."

Unnecessary, but Emily said it anyway. She still couldn't shake her suspicion, though that might have something to do with her getting pulled into all of this so quickly. Now that she had all the facts, wasn't this exactly what she had always wanted? A mission with purpose? A chance to be a hero, just like her father?

"I was trying to show you the connective tissues," Simone said. "How some of what you know fits together."

"I know what connective tissue is."

"Are you being hostile because of what already happened between us or because of what you're afraid will happen in the future?"

Emily stared at her, cycled through several insults, then settled on a shrug. "Both, I guess."

Simone sighed. "Once more, and hopefully for the last time. I'm sorry you're upset about my necessary actions. If that's not enough, we need to step into the elevator now."

"Do you have someone else if I go?"

"Of course," Simone said. "I'd be a lousy leader if I didn't have a Plan B. Or twenty other contingencies."

Emily had another sarcastic barb on the tip of her tongue but decided to let it go. Too easy. Instead, she drummed every finger on her knee a dozen times while Simone stared at her, but she couldn't make herself answer either way. She needed to trust Simone but couldn't. Was dying to take the mission but didn't want to perish as a pawn in a game she didn't understand.

"How do we know the contest isn't a trap?"

"We don't," Simone admitted.

"So, we're not just invisible. We're expendable, too."

"That's correct," she said without apology.

Emily could see the whole thing as if it had already happened. Simone was a traitor who was going to get her killed. She was being set up for a fall in some way. A scapegoat, or more likely, an alternate target to serve as distraction. Maybe both.

"You should have told me this was a suicide mission."

"You should assume that about all of them."

Simone had her there.

"When do I get to hear where we're going?" Emily asked.

"Are *we* going?"

"You already made me say I was in."

Simone stood. "It's been a long day. We could both use some sleep."

"Yes, *we're* going." Emily stood a second behind her. "But to *where*?"

"We're flying to Florida in the morning."

"What's in Florida?"

"A rendezvous at The Breakers Hotel. That's all we know. Calling the place tells us nothing. There's a party for the Uniform Ensemble Company, and we have a room paid for in their block."

"We have a reservation? Under what name?

For the first time, Simone looked embarrassed. "BullZi, with a capital Z and ending with I."

She should look embarrassed. Emily sure as hell was. "That's for me or whoever my replacement would be."

"It is. We have no idea what will happen when we get there. It could be a slaughter. It could be the first in a series of stops before getting to the real destination. Could be any one of a million other things. No way to know until we get there."

Emily took a deep breath.

Simone rushed to continue. "Don't worry about that. I doubt there would be a public slaughter at The Breakers, but yes, you are otherwise correct. So, are you going to trust me?"

"Yes," Emily lied.

"Then it's time for some shuteye."

"Here?" Emily looked around for a couch. Even a recliner.

"We're spending the night at the hotel by the airport. Need to hop on an early flight. Might as well not lose sleep to drive time."

And though she didn't want to give Simone credit for thinking of it, Emily was grateful.

Despite Simone being only a few years older than Emily, she mother-henned her, leading her to the elevator, telling her to set her alarm for 0500, suggesting things she might want to pack. The last was laughable, as she wasn't allowed to go home or to a store. At least she had a go-bag in her car, and Simone made a call to have it retrieved for her.

Everything else Simone chattered about was old information — some of it recycled to sound kinder, a shred of it a touch condescending, and the rest like a mosquito buzzing by Emily's ear.

Side by side, they walked out the door and into a darkness illuminated only by the bulb above the shack's entrance and a few similar spotlights dotting the path back toward the mess hall. Emily pretended there wasn't a hornet's nest of tension between them. But her gut was roiling, from the past or present she still wasn't sure, but she couldn't ignore it.

She had to do something. But what? So, she walked in silence, pushing the brisk pace, her mind moving even faster.

Simone led them to a waiting SUV. Someone was already standing outside with Emily's go-bag. She didn't even want to ask how they'd gotten into her car without the keys. Just took the duffel and murmured her thanks.

When she climbed in, she was surprised to find Tepper in the middle row. She wasn't surprised that her two guards were in the front. Simone pushed her to the back before claiming the bucket seat beside the director.

"I had the same idea as you," Tepper said. "I've risen with the sun since before my stint in the Army, but 0500 is early even for me."

"Are you coming with us?" Relief sluiced through Emily's veins. With Tepper there, she could relax. Simone wouldn't be able to pull the wool over her eyes.

"Negative, agent."

And just like that, Emily's tension ramped up to the red zone.

Tepper didn't offer more information about her destination, and no one had the courage to ask. Instead, the director looked over her shoulder. "I trust all your questions were answered to your satisfaction?"

How to answer that question?

"We covered a lot of ground tonight. I know I have to get up early, but I want to sleep on everything before I form an opinion of my own."

After a long, intense, unreadable stare, Tepper said, "I recognize evasion when I see it, agent. I fucking invented it. I'm not going to push you. But if you're in this car, that means you're in this mission. Understood?"

"Yes, ma'am."

"Special Agent Bisset?" She turned to the woman beside her. "Are we going to have any issues?"

"No, ma'am."

"Better not." Tepper faced front.

No one spoke again.

Check in was fast and uneventful. Emily didn't mean to eavesdrop, but she couldn't help overhearing Tepper get the suite. Her security detail didn't ask for rooms of their own. They were probably staying with her, sleeping in shifts, one dozing on the couch while the other stood guard. They headed to the elevator as she and Simone approached the desk. Then a few minutes later, Emily was sliding her keycard into the reader to unlock her door.

Simone was right across the hall.

Neither said goodnight before crossing their respective thresholds.

Emily was wired. When she'd gotten ready for work that morning, she'd had foolishly optimistic hopes — as she always did — that her day would be more fulfilling than filling out forms, filing, and fighting the urge to punch Brasse in the face for his awkward, unwanted attempts at flirting. But she'd never expected this.

Questions plagued her. Doubts ate at her.

She couldn't sleep. Couldn't settle.

Couldn't trust Simone.

She stared at the ceiling. Turned on the television, channel surfed, gave up and turned it off. Paced.

Finally, she took her wallet from her bag. Took a worn photo from the zipper compartment. Ran her finger over the strong jaw, proud smile, kind eyes.

Dad.

God, how she'd love to talk to him, bounce ideas off him. He'd know what she should do.

But she'd been denied the benefit of his wisdom for years. Denied his laughter, his love.

Denied any closure because his body had never been found.

Emily swiped at tears that should never have fallen. She kissed the photo then returned it to the safety of her wallet.

He might not be there to advise her, but she knew he wouldn't stand to leave things as they were. So, she tried to put herself in his shoes.

What would Dad do about all these doubts?

She grabbed her keycard, slipped into the hall. Eased

her door closed while staring at Simone's door for any signs of movement.

Pulse racing, she headed for the elevator. The ding when the car arrived seemed to echo down the walls. She wheeled around, stared down the corridor. When Simone didn't open her door, Emily breathed a small sigh of relief and cursed herself for not taking the stairs.

She hurried into the elevator. As the doors slid closed, her finger hovered over the buttons. P or G? Penthouse or ground floor? Answers or AWOL?

Emily pressed the button. The car jolted. The ride was smooth until it jerked to a halt. Then the doors opened with another ring of the bell.

Taking a deep breath, she steeled herself. Stepped out of the car. Headed down the hall.

Knocked.

One of the guards, still in his suit, answered before she rapped twice.

Was it Frick or Frack? They looked practically identical, making it impossible to tell. Not that she'd ever been told their names, anyway. She decided it was Frick.

He stared down at her. "What?"

"I need to talk to Director Tepper."

"She's indisposed." Frack's voice was gravelly as he stepped to the door, blinking too rapidly but otherwise looking completely alert. His pants and shirt weren't even rumpled, but his jacket and tie were off, and his top button was open, revealing just how thick his neck was.

Emily was rethinking which button she'd pressed in the elevator. She chewed her lip and considered turning around.

"It's all right."

Frack turned toward his boss. Frick still stared down at Emily, but he spoke to the director. "Ma'am, it's—"

"I know what time it is. Give us the room, please."

Frick glared at her as he stepped into the hall. Frack stifled a yawn as he brushed past her, the "accidental" elbow-to-elbow contact a bit rougher than necessary. Emily fought the urge to rub her arm as the director gestured her in.

When the door shut behind her with a decisive click, she chanced a glance at the director.

Tepper's severe bangs framed a confusion that was quickly sharpening into something else.

"I'm sorry to bother you," Emily said.

"Save the sorry and get to the why."

"We need to talk."

"Then *say something.*" Tepper glared at her.

"It's about Simone."

Somehow, Tepper's face grew harder.

Emily hurried to continue. "I think she might be up to something."

The director straightened, and her face grew grave. "Am I hearing things right now?"

"No." Emily's heart beat faster.

"Am I seeing things?"

"No." She shook her head. "Of course not."

"Am I to believe that you're standing at my door long past shuteye when we both need to wake ungodly early to tell me your handler has something to seriously worry about?"

"But that's just the thing—"

"Bisset knows exactly what she's doing. That's why *she* is your *handler.* If she didn't speak so highly of you and insist you would be willing to leave history behind you, even without the breathing time we were hoping for, I would pull the plug on you right now. Do you get that? She went to bat for you, and you're here trying to throw her under the bus."

"That's exactly the issue. I have con—"

"Instead, Agent Wyatt, I suggest you get yourself a good night's sleep. Or what's left of it. And as you nod off, it would behoove you to remember the reason I chose the pair of you is because she's a nobody and you're less than that. Neither of you is on anyone's radar but mine. And I have eyes on you both. Are we clear?"

"Crystal." Emily held her head high, just like Daddy would want her to.

"Then good night, Agent. We'll see you on the other side."

Tepper opened the door.

Frick and Frack barged in before she could exit. The second she was able, she slinked past them. And this time, when the door closed, it was with a bang.

Her heart sitting on the floor of her chest, Emily walked back to her room, terrified she had made an obviously wrong decision.

And feeling totally, utterly alone.

Chapter Four

THE TRIP to the airport was miserable.

Emily should have expected it, but she fell for the ruse. Again. Simone was all smiles as they climbed inside the Suburban — which, other than the two of them and the driver, was empty. No Tepper. No Frick and Frack.

No buffer.

Everything changed once they started rolling.

Their driver raised the partition, then Simone tore into Emily. "I asked if you trusted me and you said *yes*."

Emily swallowed. "I had to make sure."

"So, you went to Tepper and snitched on me, even though you couldn't possibly have anything to say?"

"Technically, there was no snitching. But just because I can't see the smoke doesn't mean I can't smell it." Still, she felt like a fool.

"Then tell me what you smell, Emily. Even yesterday, I still wanted to believe in you. But now it's hard not to see I've made a mistake."

"It's not too late to turn back."

"I should drop you off on the side of the road right now, but we need two for this plan to work."

"You have a replacement."

"It's a little late for that," Simone said.

"You would have done the same."

"No, Emily. I wouldn't have."

For twenty minutes, neither said anything.

Emily finally swallowed her pride and broke the silence. "I'm sorry. I shouldn't have gone to Tepper."

Simone didn't respond.

Minutes later, she tried again. "I said I was sorry."

"I see how that should make everything instantly better."

Now Emily really was feeling guilty. "What can I do?"

"I don't know, Emily. Try telling me what you're actually suspicious of. Something specific. Beyond the thing I did to recruit you. So—"

"*I'm sorry.*"

"—you could have the opportunity you always wanted. I accept your apology, but we're done talking for now." A moment later, she muttered, "Too bad we can't choose our seats on the flight."

Maybe that was something Emily could do.

And she tried the moment the opportunity presented itself. After suffering through the silence of security, shoes removed like all the other slobs without any clearance, then the trek to their gate, Emily left Simone to stand in line for a seat change.

But she couldn't get one, no matter how much she argued.

"Unless you want to purchase a first-class ticket or find another passenger who wants to switch with you, there's nothing I can do. I'm sorry."

A young man approached the counter. Handsome,

with wild hair and excited eyes. An easy smile that belied a man who was used to getting his way. Emily and the attendant had paused their conversation, both of them obviously waiting to see what this man had to say.

After a moment of uncertainty, he finally leaned forward with his elbows on the counter. In a whisper that felt like he was about to deliver a promise, the man said, "I don't mean to interrupt, but I couldn't help overhearing you two, and I think maybe there's something I can do."

"Yes, Mr. Hicks," the attendant said.

Apparently, they were on a first name basis.

"I overheard you saying there were still first-class tickets available. I'm assuming we could move a few seats around to make sure I had an attractive seat mate. Not that this is all about looks, I'm also looking for someone who knows how to maintain her composure in a frustrating situation. That's who I'd like to be sitting next to in the event of a—"

"We don't like to joke about that, Mr. Hicks," the attendant said, cutting him off.

"Understood." He nodded. Then he flashed an oh-so-charming smile, flustering the attendant. Her fingers fluttered near the charm of her necklace, and her cheeks flamed. A soft chuckle escaped him. "So, can you help me help this young woman?"

"Oh, that's okay." Emily shook her head, immune to his tactics. This was clearly a line, she couldn't be less interested, and she didn't take handouts.

Mr. Hicks turned his smile on her. "It's my pleasure."

"It's generous, thank you. But I can't accept. I'm fine where I am, really."

"Please. My family spoils me. It isn't even my money. I'll never see the bill. Let me help. You don't even have to talk if you don't want to, though I'd love to get to know you at least a little bit, if you're agreeable to the idea."

Mr. Hicks surprised her by being such a gentleman, but still, she should refuse his offer. If Emily hadn't glanced back right then and saw Simone staring back at her with both nostrils flaring, she probably would have.

"I'll take the seat if you let me buy you a drink on the flight."

He whispered as though it were a secret. "Drinks are included in first class."

"Oh, right." A nervous burble of laughter escaped her as she cast another glance at Simone.

She couldn't go back to her now, so Emily stood beside Mr. Hicks — "Rick, please," he said with a smile — and slowly got to know him. He was pleasant enough, once the awkwardness of those first few moments was behind them. But he was awfully chatty, and Emily wondered if she'd made the wrong decision.

Stony silence with Simone or nonstop prattle with Rick?

Too late to change her mind. Pretty sure she wouldn't want to, anyway.

"Do you like to fly?" Rick asked, but he continued without waiting for Emily to answer. "I love to fly. Some folks hate it, though I never understood that. I'm at home in the sky. Fourteen-hour flight, no problem. I can watch two movies and take a ten-hour nap between them. You feel me?"

"Flying is okay. I'm always glad when I land."

"Exactly! You're up in the clouds where man shouldn't be, then *BAM*, you're back down on the ground. What do you love most, besides landing?" He laughed like that last part was funny.

"I guess it's a chance to disconnect. People bitch about it, but I like that we have to turn our phones off. We're always connected, so it's nice to unplug for a little while."

"And the food is good."

Emily looked at Rick like he was crazy. "Maybe in first class it is."

"Or if you're hungry. Sometimes I can't fly first class, you know. I still like them little sam'iches and snacks. I love those waffle cookies, too — you ever eat one of those? That's a sky-high gourmet experience. Ever met anyone interesting on a plane? Or famous? I've seen a few famous folks, myself."

"Like who?"

"Saw Logan White twice. But I also sat next to the guy who owns the Night Cafe."

"What's that?"

"A chain of restaurants. You never heard of it?"

Emily shook her head.

"Apparently it's big in the Midwest. For five hours, that guy talked all about the restaurant business. It's amazing the shit you can learn if you listen."

Emily looked at him, unsure if she should ask her next question. Then she figured, why the hell not? "Would you mind my asking what your family does?"

The question seemed to take Rick by surprise.

Emily explained. "It's just that you said your family had a lot of money, but you seem … nice."

"Nice. Thanks. I think."

"I mean, not stuffy. I picture old family money and bitter siblings who don't know how to laugh or smile."

Rick did both right there in front of her. "Live without either of those and you might as well be dead already. You ever hear of Kathmandu?"

"The capital of Nepal?"

"The retailer specializing in imported home furnishings and high-end decor. Has a sorta global look."

"Like Pier One?"

"Almost exactly. Except at ten times the price." He winked.

"That's your family's company?"

"Yep. Dad thought he could do it better. He was right. The business took off. Now, here we are, first-class seat mates.

They boarded their flight a few minutes later. Emily pretended she didn't know Simone as she passed them to take her seat in the back, glaring without being too obvious. Still, she could smell the anger on her.

Rick stayed chatty, but he was good for Emily's ego. She complained in generalities, and he took her side every time. Or at least he managed to make it seem like he did.

"Sounds like your life is poorly cast," Rick had said in response to her grumbling about Simone. She'd probably gone on longer than necessary, but she hadn't been specific and had to make up three different people and scenarios to prove her irrelevant point.

By the time they landed in Palm Beach, Emily was looking forward to more of the silent treatment from Simone. Virginia to Florida wasn't an especially long flight, but with only the occasional moment empty of Rick's incessant rambling, Emily felt tired of mindlessly nodding and saying, "Uh huh."

But first class debarked together, and both travelers had baggage to claim.

While they stood together — because Rick wouldn't have it any other way — he continued to talk her ear off. Still, she didn't miss Simone as she rode down the escalator. A blind person could see she was seething. Emily refused to make eye contact as she waited for her bag. She gave Rick a fake number without even a twinge of guilt — if she couldn't even call her mom, he was definitely shit out of luck — then watched him go. As an olive branch, she grabbed Simone's bag from the carousel then circled around toward Ground Transportation to find her.

"I can't believe you let your guard down in front of a civilian," Simone said instead of *Hello*.

"I can't believe you had to fly coach."

"You're an embarrassment to this mission."

"Give me a target and we'll see about that."

Simone went back to the silent treatment.

Neither spoke as they stood in line for their rental car, nor while they drove to the rendezvous point. Emily wanted to ask when and where they were supposed to retrieve their weapons, but she didn't. Still, she longed to feel the gun in her hand. Home, whenever she could get there.

They had an afternoon to kill but nowhere to go and nothing to talk about. Simone seemed to be driving around without any particular destination.

Emily couldn't contain the question any longer. "When do I get my gun?"

"When it's ready." She kept driving. Kept not speaking.

An hour or so later, Simone got a text saying the weapons were ready and given an address for the drop. Two cases, each one with a combination they had picked out earlier. An M24. Bolt action, feeding from a detachable box magazine holding ten rounds. Able to fire machine-gun-grade ammunition, not that Emily would be foolish enough to trade speed for accuracy. Plus, a Beretta. Just in case.

They inspected their weapons, put them together then took them apart. Satisfied, they placed the pieces back into the cases. Then, still mostly silent, Simone drove around for another two hours. She went to a drive-through so they didn't have to leave their guns in the car. Another hour later, it was finally time to slip into character.

Simone got a text on the way to the meet. She frowned. "There's been a venue change."

"There has, huh?"

Shaking her head, she sighed and handed over the phone. "See for yourself."

Emily stared at the message. There was no sign of Simone lying about it. Nor would there be. Regardless, she couldn't begin to guess why the change had been made.

Unless, of course, it was a set-up.

Simone parked a few blocks from the Japanese Gardens, then they walked the remainder of the way to their rendezvous, about thirty miles away from the Breakers. Each carried her cache of weapons past the pair of heavily armed guards at the front then down the path. To either side of the walk stood pagodas, dimly lit by lanterns flickering inside them, throwing shadows on the stepping-stones that went from the shore to a tiny island in the center of a dignified pond.

The place had six gardens and one teahouse, but neither Emily nor—

Emily nearly plowed into Simone when she stopped short on the path.

A second later, Emily saw why.

Would-be contestants huddled near a raised platform that had been dressed as a stage. Rick stood at the edge of the crowd. They could see him although he wasn't yet aware of them.

"What do we do?" Emily was as shocked as she was horrified.

"What we shouldn't have done is consort with the competition back in Virginia."

Too late for that now. "Do you think he was messing with us? Could he have known who we were ahead of time?"

"How could he?" Simone stared at Rick rather than looking at Emily. "We were an hour outside of Langley. One of the few places in the world where this could possibly feel like less of a coincidence. Your friend Rick might have been moving from his latest target right to the contest."

"Is that really—"

Rick turned and spotted them. His gaze landed on Emily, and for a strobing moment of visible emotions, he seemed both baffled and adrenalized. His body almost lurched forward, but he composed himself quickly. Then he walked toward them. Almost compelled, like he was a magnet and the pair of them ore.

"Did you follow me here?" His voice was playful, though it now held a menace it hadn't before. His eyes were almost accusing, a bead of orange in each of them thanks to those flickering lanterns.

"Of course not," Emily said without thinking. "Apparently, we're in the same club."

Rick continued to look at them suspiciously.

Simone held out a hand and offered her name. A real one. "I'm Simone. This is Emily."

"That's what it said on her ticket." Rick smiled, more than a trace of misgivings still on his lips.

"When does this thing start?" Emily changed the subject.

She didn't know how many among the three of them were playing a game — it was at least her and Simone — but they all seemed grateful for the hop in topics, even if the jump was all a facade. They talked about the smallest things, their stories full of vagaries and shaded truths. Assassins assembled around them. Emily was sure she saw Garfield, maybe glimpsed Cosmo. Screencaps and that pile of photos on Simone's desk were assembled in real life. The garden air had the feeling of a bomb about to blow.

"You know Salsa?"

She didn't know if Rick meant Mexican gravy, the dance, or something else.

When Emily didn't respond, he added, "Guess not. He's uncivilized. I suggest you do not get to fucking with him. I'll be back, wanna go say hi. Motherfucker takes shit personally if he thinks he's being snubbed."

Rick had dropped three times as many curses before walking away than he had during their entire flight. Either he was really tamping it down before or a gathering of assassins brought out the potty mouth in him.

Simone was on Emily the second he fell out of earshot.

"What the hell is your problem? You never should have—"

"How was I supposed to know?"

"You decided to take the chance," Simone reprimanded her. "What was he like — are we being played?"

"Like you said, I don't see how."

"This is unacceptable. We're compromised."

"You don't know that."

"It's safe to assume we are."

"So what? We go back with nothing? Our cover's blown so we're done with the Bureau, at least when it comes to the RICO case against the Outfit? You don't want that, and neither do I."

"We could jeopardize everything by staying here," Simone said. "This is bigger than us."

"Who can come in and take our place? Right now, with no prep? We're the Bureau's only option. We should see where this goes."

"You need to get out of here."

"Excuse me?"

"I'll take the contract on my own and square things with Tepper."

"I'm not leaving," Emily said.

"I'm not giving you a choice. You need to go. I'll run damage control. Your presence complicates the situation."

"Like hell it does."

"You're a danger to the mission if you stay."

"The mission's in trouble if I leave. What's he going to think if I just disappear?"

"I don't know. That I fucking killed you?"

Emily glared. "If I'm a danger to this mission, then so are you."

"Both of us here will make this worse," Simone said. "I'm pulling rank. You're out of here."

"I'll go over your head and call Tepper."

"Your phone's a burner, she won't pick up. A conversation is impossible. And good luck coming up with a voicemail that makes you sound sane. You're done but not out. Go home. We'll pick up where we left off later, Emily. I've got my eyes on Rick. We'll salvage what we can, and I'll abort if I have—"

"Please, Simone—"

"That's an order, Wyatt."

Simone walked away, leaving Emily alone, heart pounding.

She didn't want to leave immediately, didn't want to draw attention to herself. She would drift through the crowd all the way to its edge, slip into the dark, then disappear inside the evening's many shadows.

Halfway through the crowd, someone gently grasped her arm then turned her around.

"Are you trying to ignore me?" Rick asked.

"Not at all. How was Salsa?"

"A total asshole. The man has no social grace. Farted

right in front of me a few minutes ago, and it sounded wet. It's still probably best if you don't get too near the guy. He has a sort of 'if I see it, I'm allowed to fuck it' attitude. You know the type." Rick shrugged and looked at Emily. "Where's your friend? Simone."

"It looks like we're parting ways."

"Oh?" Rick raised his eyebrows.

"Yeah. We have history."

"She one of the people on the plane you were making up?"

"What makes you think I was making anything up?" Emily asked.

"I thought so then. Now that I know what you do for a living, I'm sure of it."

"You're assuming a lot."

He shrugged again. "Doubt I'm wrong. And now Miss Princess has ditched you. Probably figured she could win this game by herself, no alliances necessary. So that leaves more for me." A wink at Emily. "And don't think it's because of what you look like. You're all right, but it ain't that. You made me laugh a dozen times during our flight, and I did most of the talking. All lies have some truth in 'em, and I have a good idea about what you were saying in your stories."

"What was I saying?" Emily asked.

"You don't want to be alone."

Rick's answer surprised her enough, but then he shocked Emily harder.

"And you shouldn't be. Adios, Miss Princess. Hello, Mr. Hicks. We're gonna have us a good time at the old show tonight."

"Sorry, I hated my last partner." Emily shook her head. "Turned me off for good. It's solo or bust."

"You say that, but that's emotion talking. You're not

thinking clearly. Being by yourself right now don't make a lick o' sense. My goal is to get to the end. Easier to do if I have someone watching my back. We can worry about shooting each other later."

"Why don't you already have a partner, if you wanted one?"

"I've got options."

"Is Salsa on the list?" Emily didn't even know why she was asking.

"Of course not. That man is a savage. I'd call him a low alternate. Look, my plan was to go solo and see where this went. But I like to think of myself as the sort to pay attention, and in that case, maybe this is where it was supposed to go. You and me, until one of us has to blow the other's brains out. You're toned and well-trained, if even half your stories are based on something real. Like I said, them odds are hot."

Emily considered. There was a lot to like about working with him. Yes, it was an excellent way to get information on the competition and the Outfit itself. Salsa was proof Rick apparently knew more than they did, at least about some things. It would be natural for him to share with his partner. Faking a kill would be difficult, but maybe she could turn him. Or beat Rick to all the targets.

"We'll see," Emily said.

She would have said *yes*, but a new energy rippled through the crowd. All eyes turned toward the front as a bare-chested man dressed in only yoga pants appeared on a rock platform before them. He didn't seem to have a hair on his body.

Emily didn't know how long the man had been there. Or how he got there at all. To her, his arrival looked like a magic trick.

"Good evening everyone. I am your host, Amil."

A Simple Kill

A wave of mutters rumbled through the crowd as all eyes faced front.

"I'm sure many of you were hoping to see the Foreman, but that will not happen until the end of our competition. I'm also certain you are all eager to get started, as is the Foreman. According to our headcount, all registered participants are now in attendance. Given the stakes, we should get started immediately. Please, indulge in the appetizers — Gyoza, spicy edamame, and chicken scallion skewers. Next to the plates, you will each find a tablet with your name on it. This is where you will 'show your work,' so please keep the tablet with you at all times. It is the only approved device to record your kills or any other action where you expect to receive points."

Other actions?

Amil took a moment to survey the crowd. "Finished tasks are worth one hundred points, eliminated henchmen are worth fifteen. Organization heads are good for fifty, and creativity or artistry in problem-solving will add an additional fifty points to your score."

Artistry?

Rick leaned over and whispered, "Salsa will clean up there."

"Please, eat. In fifteen minutes, your first target will be announced."

And then he rang a bell.

Chapter Five

THE ENERGY CHANGED IMMEDIATELY.

Amil stopped talking. With the simple act of ringing a bell, the world suddenly felt different.

The group was still civilized, but its ire had been collectively raised. Emily could smell the testosterone. Sniper School was full of the scent. But now it permeated her senses in an oddly specific way and made her miss the comfort of Simone.

Now, Emily was on a long walk with Rick. And she wasn't even sure where they were headed. He liked to "think while he walked," so they left the Japanese Gardens. She was pretty sure he was wandering without any particular direction or destination in mind. As much as she hated the unknown, she asked questions and feigned interest. Played the partner role as best she could despite not ever officially committing to becoming a team.

The farther she got from the rest of the group, the more she missed Simone. It wasn't an expected, or even welcome, emotion. Still, Emily couldn't ignore the truth — given their current circumstances, Simone would help her feel safe. Fortunately, she and Rick were on a brightly lit street, with more than a handful of people in plain sight. A trio of teenagers walked out of the 7-Eleven up ahead, each sipping a Slurpee through a bright blue straw. Across the street, couples held hands as they strolled down the sidewalk, occasionally sharing a quiet laugh or exchanging shy smiles. A middle-aged man stepped out of the liquor store, hefting a box with way too many bottles for a New Year's Eve party let alone a random evening at home.

Yeah, the public street provided an element of safety. But only a small one.

Rick could easily kill her the second he decided to. One turn into an alleyway or anywhere thick with shadows, and that would be that. Emily was an ace from her side of a sniper rifle, one of the best behind a scope, but hand-to-hand with this guy? Despite all her self-defense training, she didn't stand a chance.

There was no outward, obvious danger. The mood was more of a silent, menacing threat. Nothing like before, when Emily saw Rick as the Good Samaritan he was pretending to be while buying her that first class ticket. Then, she'd suspected he'd had some sort of ulterior motive. Now, she knew it. Rick wasn't a rich trust fund kid like he had wanted her to believe, that was only a story told to relax her. The real reason he had all that cash was because 'professional murder' was a lucrative gig.

His personality hadn't changed, but the context had, and now Emily saw everything through a prism of danger. Rick was a bit loud and slightly off-color. That morning, she had seen those traits as belonging to a kid in an adult's body, to a man who had never really needed to grow up thanks to family wealth and connections. But now Emily saw his behavior for what it was — the arrogant swagger of a criminal who saw himself as above the law. Despite the pleasant nature of their exchanges, they were enemies awaiting an introduction.

She longed to shed her creeping unease — the looming sense of danger making Emily feel almost brittle. They kept talking as they walked, unearthing a plan together. Every once in a while, Rick would look over, and a gleam in his predatory eyes would send a chill through her body. Emily would ignore it, keep putting one foot after the other, pretend she hadn't shat the bed by angering her handler and potentially putting the mission in danger by pairing herself with a professional assassin.

It was all a matter of perspective. Hard to take exception to his profession when it was hers, too. And she had never wanted to be anything else, had always been determined to follow in her father's footsteps.

But there was a difference between them. Rick was there to apply for a job with the Outfit. Probably worked for a number of horrible people doing horrible things … for anyone willing to pay him. His kind of hitman had no conscious. He was a mercenary willing to work for the highest bidder. On the other hand, Emily and her father worked for the United States Government to rid the world of evil like Rick and the Outfit. She was there to ultimately stop the carnage, not to add to it.

But she had made her bed. So, for now, Rick really was on her team. She couldn't be halfway there. As long as she and Rick walked side-by-side, Emily had to be all the way in and stay there for as long as she could. If he so much as smelled the betrayal on her, she'd likely end up with a bullet in the back of her skull. Or worse.

They were sorting the details, figuring out how to get the job done better and faster than everyone else. Amil had explained it all in simple enough terms. The Outfit had wrestled control of a rather significant pipeline of coke and heroin running from Cuba to Miami. Now someone was trying to usurp their position. The contestants were there to make sure that didn't happen.

The mission was straightforward, but that didn't make it simple or easy. They had to intercept the shipment and teach the competition a lesson. It was that last part Rick was looking forward to most. Enough to cackle when he talked about it.

But this was out of Emily's wheelhouse. Her experience was in marksmanship, battlefield intelligence, and other sniper-related skills. Long-range precision fire. More to the point, she was supposed to fake it all and not actually do it. None of this was what she had been trained to do. At all.

Rick, on the other hand, was in his element. And loving it. He was suggesting something closer and much more personal than sniper fire, preferably using knives.

"Ain't nothing to be afraid of," he said, when she pushed back yet again.

"I just don't see the benefit to getting so close."

But he appeared to excavate joy by needling Emily into arguing her point.

"I'm not afraid, Rick. But I'm also not stupid. We can eliminate our targets from farther away."

"I get why you like your sniper rifles, sunshine. The job's a lot more dangerous up close. But it is what it is, and I'll argue myself cobalt that right now we got no other choice. We don't have enough information to set up shop from far away. We don't even know which cargo container we're looking for."

"We're on the ground to figure that out," Emily argued.

"Tick-tock, sweetheart. If we're in this to win this, then we gotta strike first. You do you, but I'm planning on killing every fucker but one, then I'm sending the surviving peon back to the Foreman with piss still dribbling down his leg. You can stay in the Honeycomb Hideout if you want, and I'll still consider us partners. Maybe you get to shoot some fuckers from far away the next time while I get to kick it. Who cares? This time, we take the money and the shipment back to Amil, then boom goes the cherry bomb and we're the winners for round one."

"That's very generous of you. And stupid," Emily dared.

"Pardon my fuck you?"

She had done something absurd. Reckless, stupid. Ditching her handler was a knee-jerk reaction. Simone might be a traitor, but Rick was one-hundred percent a criminal void of even the pretense of civility. Emily had been so worried about Simone's betrayal, she'd hooked up with someone who would kill her without flinching. And worse, doing her job now would be that much more difficult. She couldn't communicate with Simone or Tepper. Even if she did learn something valuable, that knowledge might be lost. Along with her life.

"I have no problem taking care of business on the ground, but I need a reason beyond your testosterone." Emily stopped, drew a breath, used everything inside herself to stare him down. "I plan on winning this, which means if you'd like to land in second place, you might want to listen. Or we could each do our own thing. No reason to keep working together just because we've started."

"What do you propose?" The question felt oddly like a courtesy.

"We each do what we do best. Divide and conquer. You get the shipment and the money. I'll handle the people. We just need to know the cargo containers. I can still go down and try to charm—"

"Nah," Rick cut her off. "I know a guy who can get what we need."

"How?"

"He's a hacker. Always on call. And fast."

"Why didn't you say that before?"

"He's expensive. I was trying to save money."

"You weren't trying to save money," Emily dared again. "Are you planning on doing anything else this stupid while we're working together? We needed shipping info and container numbers. You know a hacker who can get that for us, but you—"

"I like a challenge. But you're right. And as proof, I already said it. *Tick-fucking-tock.*"

"I don't think we should approach the shipping container at all."

Rick stopped walking and stared at her. They had gone back and forth about what to do on the ground for a while now. But this was a brand-new argument.

"That's what everyone is going to do. Most of us have hackers at our disposal—"

"You don't." Rick laughed.

"—so the information is out there. The yard will be packed with our competition. I think we should intercept the boat while it's still in the water instead of ambushing them on the docks. Get the jump on everyone."

"No way, sunshine."

"Stop calling me sunshine."

"We need the shipment and the money. One of them ain't gonna cut it."

"That's what all the idiots think, which is why the shipping yard will be full of them. Read between the lines. What would the Foreman really want? Sure, the money would be nice, but it ain't like the Outfit is hurting. The drugs are half the value, but the real benefit here? A disruption to the pipeline and a powerful message sent. Bloodbaths are bad for business. This is the best move."

"It's a hard-fucking left is what it is."

"It's the right strategy, and you know it. Remember, creativity points. And my plan has 'ingenuity' written all over it."

Rick paused, considered for a moment, then nodded. "Well, all right then. I'll get in touch with Toejam."

That had to be the hacker, but Rick didn't say, and she didn't ask.

He took out his phone, put it to his ear. Started to walk off in the other direction as the conversation began.

She was glad they stopped. Her arms were throbbing. Rick had offered to carry her gun case, but he had a better chance of her carrying his baby.

His departure gave her the perfect opportunity to contact Simone. Not wanting to make noise, she chose not to call but to just send a text.

Contact the Coast Guard. The only way to prevent massive casualties is to stop the ship from reaching PortMiami. Will text you shipping and cargo info when I have it, but contact CG now.

Then she waited.

And waited.

Rick would be back any second. Should have been back already. But she'd lost sight of where he went and couldn't track him. All she knew for sure was it was too risky to try Simone again.

So, she kept waiting. Until she couldn't stand it. Sent another message, pulse racing. Palms so slick with sweat, she nearly dropped her phone.

Text me back to let me know you got this.

Maybe Simone wasn't getting the texts. Emily should probably call her.

Except she had no idea where Rick was, and if he circled back and found her talking to—

No, she could always make up a story. Buy herself some time.

But how often could she pull a trick like that before he put a few bullets in her? She could imagine it now, Rick laughing while he emptied his gun.

Couldn't help herself. Tried one last time.

Please.

Still nothing.

Emily swallowed. Her heart was pounding. But she was desperate. So, she dialed.

It went straight to voicemail. Her mouth was open, ready to start speaking a second after the beep, but as soon as Simone's voice mail kicked on, Emily heard a heckling voice behind her.

"Hey there, sunshine."

Chapter Six

HE'D TAKEN Emily to a luxury condo, overlooking the water.

"You just happened to have a safe house in Miami?" Emily asked.

"Sure do."

"Does this place belong to you, or is it a timeshare you have with other assassins?"

"It's kinda sorta both. Mostly mine, though."

"Mostly yours, huh? I don't care how good you are at your job, this is a lot for someone your age. Especially since I'm assuming Miami isn't the only city where you have a place like this. Maybe you're stretched a little thin, and that's why you were trying to save money on a hacker."

Rick shrugged. "I told you, my family has a lot of scratch."

"Oh, right. Kathmandu. Not the capital of Nepal, but a 'retailer specializing in imported home furnishings and decor. For a sorta global look.' Like Pier One."

He grinned. "Your memory continues to impress me."

"Your story is bullshit."

"It ain't. My family owns the Kathmandu chain."

"And you're an assassin? Why?"

Rick smirked. "Because it's fun."

"I can't tell if you're full of shit."

"Makes no difference to me what you believe, sunshine. Just make sure I don't get killed. I take it you don't have a safe house here in Miami. What were you planning on doing without the benefit of my hospitality? Twice now today."

"I had a place to go."

"Then why aren't we there?"

"One, you took me here. Two, I'm willing to trust you for one night because right now it's not in your best interests to kill me. Three, this place is a lot nicer than mine would be, and I would have had to call in a favor to get it. And four, this works out better for me, so I accepted your oh-so-generous offer."

"Then you're welcome." His smile was more of a sneer.

That had been an hour ago. Rick left shortly after that. Said he was going to nab them a boat for the mission since they would need to hit open water before dawn. It hadn't been a discussion, and he hadn't asked Emily what she thought. He'd simply made the announcement then disappeared out the front door after trading phone numbers.

She didn't know him well enough to tell if his behavior was suspicious. There was something strange about him under the best of circumstances, even when he'd pretended to be the kind stranger upgrading her to a first-class experience.

At first, she was glad he was gone. Relieved to be alone. It gave her a chance to do a few things she'd put off in his presence. Emily checked for Simone's text, and finding none, sent her another. She cleaned her rifle then held it reverently. Cradled it, really. Then she put it away.

Sent Simone another message. And one after that.

Texted Rick, too. Just to get a sense of how long he'd be gone and what he'd found.

No answer from him, either.

Tried a few more times. Same result.

A second hour passed. The safe house was on the water, so Rick didn't have to go far to get a boat. Where the hell was he?

Maybe rather than going right outside, he went to the docks for something more commercial. That made sense.

But he hadn't answered a single text, and it had taken her a long time to send the first one.

Something wasn't just off with Rick. Something was off with the entire situation. So why was she sitting here in this safe house if her instincts were screaming it wasn't safe?

Because that was paranoia crowing. She knew how to shut it out.

Emily took her father's photo from her wallet. Stared at it. Willed him to send her peace. And a plan.

She found neither and returned the photo to its rightful place.

After another hour, three total, with water right outside their window, Emily began to seriously worry. Not that Rick had gotten caught or that she would be compromised by his capture. She could slip out the window and climb down the balcony. This apartment had clearly been chosen for such an escape. There was always the possibility of the place being surrounded, but it felt remote. She was a nobody.

No, her worries were far greater than law enforcement.

Emily was much more concerned about being set up for something.

Three hours was a long time. Enough to move from a general suspicion to an absolute certainty that something was up. When she hit the four-hour mark, Emily refused to sit still any longer.

She had to get out of there but didn't have a car. Simone had theirs, and after their eternal walk, Rick had driven them to his place. She didn't have keys for his ride. Hell, for all she knew, he'd taken it somewhere. That left her without transportation.

Breaking away from her handler had put Emily in a constant state of danger. But that defined a sniper's life.

Maybe he had a second car. Rick seemed frivolous with money, so it was certainly possible he had more than one vehicle.

Twenty minutes. If he has a second car, I'll find the keys in under twenty minutes.

But she didn't even need two. Found what she was looking for on a corkboard by the front door.

For such a messy personality, Rick was surprisingly neat.

She grabbed the fob from the hook then went down to the parking garage, but she had no idea what kind of car she was looking for. A glance at the plastic in her hand offered no clues. Emily clicked it, listened for the beep, then followed the far-off sound up the ramp and to the right. When she rounded the corner, she clicked it again. Her jaw dropped when she saw the vehicle.

"You've gotta be fucking kidding me."

It was a Cadillac, which Emily only knew because of the emblem on its grill. The car looked like it was from the 40s, with a wide sloping body that resembled a spaceship.

A crazy-expensive, customized lowrider scraping the ground.

Emily hoped there wouldn't be anything weird about the car that she couldn't control as she opened the door. She climbed inside to find the interior had been entirely modernized. In addition to the remote entry, it had a keyless ignition. A brightly lit digital dashboard. Plush leather seats.

The chassis was old, but everything else was beautifully new.

She had nothing to worry about. The car started right up. As long as she didn't treat the thing like a lowrider, she would be fine. The GPS was intuitive, and after a minute on the road, Emily was on her way to the docks.

It was a big place with too many places to park or hide or investigate. A place where anyone might be lurking — her competitors or the people she was supposed to be taking down.

For Emily, it was the most dangerous place in the world.

People milled about, but that wasn't strange in a place like this, even at night. Made it harder to tell who should be there and who shouldn't.

After a half hour of driving the docks in Rick's Cadillac lowrider, there was still no sign of its owner. But ten minutes after that, Emily pulled over at the sight of what she swore was Simone.

It was. And even though the light was barely there, Simone seemed happy to see her.

"You look relieved."

"I am," Simone said. "I saw Rick about twenty minutes ago. He took a boat. I didn't see you with him and worried that he …"

Simone was an actress, but it was still one hell of a performance.

"I'm fine. Anything happen before he took the boat?"

"No. That's the only reason I saw him. I heard a commotion and—"

"Awfully convenient, you running into him in a place like this."

"Are we doing this again?" Simone asked.

"Do we need to?"

"We need to work together, Emily. You spent time with him. Surely you talked about some sort of plan. Tell me what it is so we can do something to stop it."

"I told you the plan! And I'm guessing you didn't contact the Coast Guard?"

"When did you tell me the plan? We just started talking! And why would I contact the Coast Guard?"

"I texted you hours ago. Many times."

"I didn't get any texts from you, and I've been checking my phone all night."

She stared at her so-called handler. Was she lying? For all Emily she knew, Simone and Rick were working together and now Emily's cover was blown.

That last thought was like a fungus refusing to leave her.

"We're attacking the shipment directly in the morning. Before it reaches the docks," Emily said, studying Simone but mining nothing from her reaction. "That's why I wanted you to contact the Coast Guard."

"Let me think," Simone said.

Emily continued to study her.

That theory refused to leave her mind. Simone and Rick really could be working together. Everything fit, even if Emily couldn't understand how or why. Too many coincidences set this whole thing in motion. Running into him at the counter by the gate. Him buying her, a random stranger, a first-class ticket out of the goodness of his heart, just for pleasant company on the flight. Simone getting pissed at her and triggering their split at the original rendezvous, prompting her to go off with Rick. Rick going off on his own to "get them a boat," and Simone being at the docks when Emily went looking for him.

That could have all been orchestrated. Simone had done something similar to Emily before. Her so-called mentor had gone behind her back at Sniper School. Befriended her male classmates and joined them in vicious hazing pranks. Worse, she'd orchestrated them. Not that Emily had realized it at the time. And when it came time for the final test? Another betrayal. Which stung all the more because they'd been more than sisters-in-arms. They'd been friends. But they hadn't. Not really.

Another lie.

She was an idiot for allowing herself to blindly walk into the same thing again.

"Are we going to stop Rick or not?" Emily asked.

"You're not working with him anymore?"

"I'm sure I blew that relationship by leaving the safe house. But I don't think that matters, because I don't think he's going back. He's going through with the attack without me, so we need to stop him."

"Maybe," Simone said.

"What do you mean, *maybe*?"

"We're not getting anywhere unless you start trusting me. Do you think I can't see the way you're looking at me right now? It's not that dark. If this is how things are going to be for good, then we don't stand a chance. So, is there anything you want to ask me?"

"What do you want me to say, Simone? There's no difference between the way you are when you're being honest and when you're lying to my face. How am I ever supposed to forget that?"

"I don't think you can. But throughout the remainder of this mission, I expect you to put it in your past enough to give me some benefit of the doubt. So again, *is there anything you want to ask me?*"

Emily clenched and unclenched her fists. "Do you think it's peculiar that Rick was on the same flight as us?"

"Of course, it is. I also think flying that close to Langley changes the odds."

"And what about my going off with him? Surely you can see why I might think that had been set up by the both of you."

"Given our history and your paranoia, absolutely."

Emily bristled.

"But why? What's my purpose?"

"You tell me."

Simone sighed. "I'm trying to catch the bad guys. And right now, we're wasting time. So—"

"How about you call the Coast Guard?" Emily interrupted.

"Tepper needs the update and calling her will get things moving faster. Plus, big bonus, you get to hear me giving our boss the rundown so you can be sure we're all on the same page."

"Then what?" Emily asked.

"Then, we steal a boat."

"It's wrong to—"

"Wrong is relative, and what's relative right now is that it's too late for us to secure a vessel any other way. We're calling the Coast Guard, and this is happening. I think Rick's headed toward the incoming boat right now."

"Why steal a boat if we're calling the Coast Guard?"

"You know that's not enough, Emily. We have a job to do."

"We can't steal someone else's prop—"

"We can make it right later. This is our most strategic move. You want to be a super soldier, start acting like—"

"But it's wrong."

"So is failing at our jobs. And the consequences of that wrong are a whole lot worse."

Emily hated how much it made her head and stomach hurt to know Simone was right.

"Fine." Emily took a torpedo-sized hit to her pride. "Let's steal a boat and get it over with."

Her phone began to buzz. Emily took it out of her pocket then glanced at the screen. Surprised, she looked up at her handler.

"Who is it?" Simone asked.

"It's Rick."

Hey there, sunshine.

Rick managed to work in her hated nickname before sending the coordinates for both the incoming boat and the cargo container. The timing was perfect, his message coming in just before Simone was about to call the colonel.

Tepper was impressed. She commended them both and made Emily feel like maybe this was worth it. Simone was right to call the colonel right in front of her. She could hear Tepper on the other line, loud enough to fill her with hope. Or something along the border of faith.

Simone hung up and looked at Emily. "Tepper said it's handled."

"So, we don't need to steal a boat."

"Nothing has changed, except now the colonel knows what we're up to. We still need to do our jobs."

"And where do you propose we get a boat?"

Simone said, "I know just the place."

It was a spot she had supposedly scoped out in anticipation of having to lift a vessel on her own. Emily found it awfully convenient that there was yet another perfect dot on a map she couldn't see yet somehow found herself following.

Simone made stealing the boat look easy. She knew exactly what she wanted, how to get her chosen boat started, and the best way to ease it out of the slip and into the ocean. She claimed it was because she had worked a case involving what was essentially a chop shop for boats. Most thieves stole the vessels for the engines because they went for as much as twenty-thousand dollars. But Emily still couldn't help but wonder if Simone really knew about that particular boat because it was all a part of some invisible plan.

The coast was barely behind them when Simone's phone began to buzz.

Emily studied her face for signs of duplicity as she put the phone to her ear, listened, soaked into what was clearly an unpleasant message, muttered a couple of questions that only made Emily more curious, swallowed hard, then finally said, "Yes, Director." She hung up the phone.

"What is it?" The night wind kissed her brow, cooling the fresh sheen of flop sweat.

"We have the wrong information. The ship, the cargo. All of it. Rick lied."

"Do you think he knows?"

"Maybe, but the sabotage makes sense either way. Even if we're only competing, of course Rick wants to win." Simone sighed and seemed to push the boat harder.

"So where are we going now?"

"To the proper coordinates."

There were a few exchanges, but it was mostly silent after that. Didn't take long before they reached the right location — a boat full of drugs surrounded by the Coast Guard.

"We're too late," Emily said.

"Or right on time."

They fell silent and surveyed what was obviously the end of a well-coordinated effort. Impressive, considering they were on the phone with Tepper a bit more than an hour ago. Three boats on the scene, having triangulated their time, speed, and distance almost perfectly. A helicopter hovered above them, spilling buckets of illumination onto the ocean and making the water look like a Hollywood backlot.

At-sea interdictions could take more than a dozen hours, and even then, the Coast Guard could come up with nothing. Sometimes it was because the suspected vessel carried no contraband. But most of the time, it was because the smugglers were smart enough to offload the swag as soon as they thought interception was likely or even possible.

It looked like the Coast Guard had been there for a while, with an initial safety sweep behind them. They would be combing the vessel for contraband.

"There." Simone nodded past the heart of commotion, away from the hovering lights, deep into the darkness.

Emily followed her gaze to another boat, bobbing in the water.

Simone aimed their vessel its way and slowly cut through the chop.

"It's Rick," Emily said before she could be absolutely certain. "I'm sure of it."

They drew their guns. Emily was surprised to see Simone already had the suppressor fixed to hers. By the time they were near enough to the other boat to recognize its occupants — Rick and a squat man with a goatee and a trucker's cap — they saw one of them was armed.

Trucker Cap had his gun aimed at Emily. He wore a sloppy grin suggesting he couldn't wait to pull the trigger.

"Well, well—"

Simone didn't let it get any further than that. She pulled the trigger and sent a bullet into his face. The BOOM was muffled, but still everything seemed to explode.

Ribbons of liquid spilled from his head, got lost in the dark. Plasma sprayed and spilled. A thunk then a splash, indicative of a body hitting the boat then falling into the water. The palpable sense of collective attention turning toward them.

Rick wasn't armed, so he raised his hands in surrender.

"What are we doing?" Emily whispered as Simone pulled closer to the other boat.

"We're boarding that one, leaving this one behind, then getting the hell out of here. If we're lucky, and I'm not saying we will be, Rick will believe we outran or outsmarted the Coast Guard. Or that they saw us as minnows after they already had their fish."

"Why do we want him?"

"We want to know what he knows," Simone said.

"I'm not coming aboard your boat." Rick laughed at them once they were near enough, then in a daring voice he added, "So I guess you're going to have to shoot me."

"You seem awfully sure that I won't."

"Coast Guard is coming over already. Seems like a bad idea to turn one curiosity into a sudden emergency."

"You're not boarding this boat, but we are getting on yours." Simone steadied her aim. "I'm happy to let you live or shoot you. Your choice."

He said nothing as Emily boarded.

She tried not to think about the bits of blood and bone her feet might be treading on. Instead, she held her weapon on him so Simone could take her turn getting on the boat.

Once she had her balance, she patted him down, just in case.

She passed Emily a Glock that had been tucked into his waistband.

She tucked it into her own. Took a deep breath. Vented it slowly. Simone had the situation — and Rick — under control. The Coast Guard could return the stolen boat to its owners. All they had to do now was get back to shore without incident. Which included keeping up the ruse.

She sucked in another deep breath.

"Where are you taking me?" Rick asked.

Simone stared out at the ocean, refusing to look at him. "To the Marina."

"So, it was you that called the Coast Guard?" Rick spat. "I should have known."

"Of course not," Emily answered him.

"They just happened to be out in the big old ocean in that exact same spot as you."

"And you," Simone said.

"You would have been scooped up with the rest of them if you weren't a part of it," Rick argued.

"You weren't," Emily cut in.

"We stayed back, out of sight. On purpose. Risky, but better than the way y'all came in there like you didn't care if you were seen."

"We came in fast because we were following the Coast Guard. We were just another boat in the water. Why would *we* be following *them* if we were criminals? They saw us as curious boaters and warned us off. So, we let the Guard get ahead of us but never lost them."

"They ain't chasing you now?"

"Why would they?" Emily asked, not believing a word she was about to say. "They didn't hear the gunshot. At best, they were aware of some commotion. But they had enough on their hands, so why divide their attention? They wouldn't. Sure, they'll investigate, I'm sure they're doing it right now. Or will soon. But they'll find a stolen boat with no one on board. The evidence is all here with us, including the bits of body your buddy left behind before he toppled into the drink. The Coast Guard will figure the thieves got away, at least until they find the body. And we'll be long gone by then. For now, we're not worth chasing since they've already landed a bigger catch."

It felt like the perfect leap when Emily took it, but she knew it was for sure after Simone caught her.

"Seems a lot more likely that asshole I shot is the one who tipped off the Coast Guard."

Simone's explanation seemed to catch Rick by surprise. "What makes you say that?"

"How well did you know him?" Emily asked.

"I asked you first."

"Why would we tip off the Coast Guard?" Simone asked. "If we *hadn't* followed them, we never would have found you. Remember? You gave us the wrong coordinates. So, one of you had to tip them off. If it wasn't you, that means it had to be your buddy. And if you don't want me suspecting you, putting a bullet in your brain, and shoving you overboard to join your friend, you'll answer my question. How well did you know him?"

"That Fucker," Rick grumbled. "Wish I'd have shot him myself. So, what's the plan?"

Simone stared at him for a long time. Then she said, "We start with you giving us one good reason not to kill you right now."

"Why would you want to do that?" Rick seemed genuinely surprised by the question. "I trust you."

Like hell, he did.

"But I don't trust you," Emily said. "You gave me the wrong information."

"It's a game! That's what I'm supposed to do. You, too. Haven't y'all ever played a game before?"

Simone reminded Rick she had a gun by waving it in his face. "I don't play games with people's lives."

"Then you're in the wrong line of work," Rick said.

Simone leaned into him. "I'm in exactly the right line of work. Because I never confuse business and games. I'm still waiting for that reason."

"Okay," Rick said with a shrug. "Nuts and bolts, you won't kill me because neither of you are stupid."

"And what makes you think it's not smart for us to kill you?" Emily asked.

"Because I have information you need to get further in this little game. So right now, I'm worth a hell of a lot more to you alive than dead. You have no real reason to kill me. I set you up to gain an advantage, but I didn't put you in any danger. A spot in the ocean? You did worse for yourselves by following the Coast Guard."

"Your partner had his gun on us," Emily said.

"You had yours on him." Rick nodded at Simone. "And she pulled the trigger."

"He was going to kill us and like it," Simone said.

Rick gave them both an acknowledging nod. "You're probably right."

"How can we ever trust you? You've already betrayed us once."

"You kidding me?" Rick looked at Emily like she was crazy. "We're not dating, and I don't owe you dick."

"You asked me to be your partner."

"An offer you never officially accepted, sunshine."

She scowled.

"I didn't betray you. Unless we made a blood oath, or a pinky promise, or some other sort of *I swear,* I never owed you the truth. I was myself on the flight before I knew who you were, not that I know who you are now. Circumstances changed when we met for the second time, and you can't argue otherwise. Same for your friend here." A nod to Simone. "There is no *us.* I don't know shit about the two of you."

"What do you know?" Simone asked.

He scoffed. "Like I'm gonna tell you. Say you'll let me live and we can start the conversation."

"How do we know you're not buying time?"

Rick rolled his eyes at Emily. "Of course, I'm buying time. That don't subtract from the value of my knowing shit. You two ladies are welcome to use the other side of this fine vessel to talk amongst yourselves. I'll be in the corner."

Emily traded a look with Simone. They were probably thinking the same thing. It was weird to be following Rick's direction. He had orchestrated that perfectly. He hadn't even issued orders, and yet they were still taking them. What else were they going to do? Not use the moment to confer?

"I don't trust him at all," Simone whispered.

"Obviously. Me neither."

"To be fair, you don't trust me."

"To be fair," Emily countered, "once upon a time you shoved a knife in my back."

"Not now. Let's keep this about Rick. What are you thinking? I already told you, I don't trust him."

"And I told you I don't trust him, either. But I do think he knows something, and I think we should figure out what that is. We both know we're not going to kill him unless we have to, so we need to keep him believing we will."

"You have more rapport. Use it to figure out what he knows," Simone said.

"Next will you please explain how to make a bowl of cereal?"

"So, what did you ladies decide?" Rick asked, raising his hands to further prove his surrender.

They stopped trading whispers.

Emily stepped front of Simone and met Rick's gaze. "Let's say we're the Three Amigos for now. What's our next move?"

He grinned. "Well, I suggest we get our money back."

Chapter Seven

"No, I don't want a drink!" Simone snapped. "And I'm not going to want one at any point in the near future, so stop asking me."

"I figured as much," Rick said. "I just didn't wanna hear you bitching about it if I failed to make her highness a drink. Either of your highnesses."

"You were saying," Emily prompted.

They were back in Rick's safe house, where he harbored quite the liquor collection.

Rick finished filling his glass full of Artemis Tull, took a quick sip, then licked his lips. "I was saying we shouldn't give up all the points. We've still got time. We went tits up on the task, so we won't be nabbing the hundred for that. But I'd say a few henchmen went down on account of the Coast Guard."

"I'm not sure that counts," Simone said.

Rick ignored her. "Regardless, there was no organization head on that boat, but there sure as hell were some henchmen, and they might count. So does creativity and artistry in problem-solving and execution. Fifty points. And artistry is where my idea shines."

"If you ever get to it," Emily said.

"She has a point."

"I'm there already. Jesus, you two are impatient." Rick took a breath, and for a second it really sounded like he was finally going to deliver his big idea. Instead, he said, "You might not like the idea, but before we get into the whats and hows of it, I need to remind you we have to do something to advance, and right now we have nothing."

"I thought we had the henchman," Simone said.

"I'm putting it out there," Rick admitted, "but we all know the henchman are a Hail Mary. If we want a guaranteed pass into the next round, we'll need us a better plan than hoping for it."

Emily hadn't even considered an elimination round. But it only made sense. If they didn't come up with something, their mission was over. It made Rick's plan their only plan, which made it even more important that he tell them what it was.

"*So, what's your idea?*" Emily glared at him, wondering if he really thought he was a good enough showman to keep stringing them along like this.

"Can we agree that we need to do something if we expect to advance?" Rick asked. It was clear that only a *yes* would get him to continue.

"Agreed," Simone said.

"And can we agree that we need to work—"

"Yes," Emily answered before he could finish. "Just spit it out already."

"We need to hit the DEA evidence room."

Simone laughed, hard.

"You can laugh all you want, but that's our best bet."

Rick looked at them, waiting for one of them to offer up a better response, or at least one not riddled in laughter.

Simone had stopped guffawing and was now staring at Rick just like Emily.

When neither of them said anything, he added to his argument. "The Coast Guard gives their seized drugs to the DEA. The DEA then saves some of those drugs for trial and destroys the rest. We want the haul before it's destroyed, that's where we'll find it. And maybe, not likely but possible, maybe we get the money, too."

Simone shook her head. "We won't get the money. Even if we were crazy enough to raid the DEA evidence room."

"Not with that attitude," Rick said.

"So, your big idea that you've made us wait all this time for while you finished an entire glass of whiskey and then started on a second one" — Emily's voice was gaining speed and pitch as she spoke — "is to break into a highly secure and heavily armed facility, ASAP, so we can finish our mission impossible before the drugs are destroyed."

"With a lot less cynicism, but yeah," Rick nodded. "That sounds about right."

"There's no way to do that," Simone said.

"Of course, there are ways. Remember ... *artistry*."

Emily took a step away from him. "You're crazy. You want to go in there guns blazing? We'll all die"

"You misunderstand me." Rick took another sip while the women watched him. "I may talk fast, but that don't make me a fast talker. I speak straight, same as I shoot, and I don't want to go in guns blazing. I suggest we slip in quiet then leave with what we need. If, however, we find ourselves in the midst of a firefight, you can best believe I will empty both barrels into any motherfuckers feeling lucky enough to stand in my way."

"You want that to happen."

He turned to Simone. "And why would I want that?"

"Because you're crazy," she told him.

"I'm not crazy at all." He laughed and tipped his chin at Emily. "Did she tell you about Salsa?"

Simone looked at Emily. *Do you know what the hell he's talking about?*

She shrugged. "He's one of the hitmen. Apparently, he's crazy."

"I think his real name is Mikey," Rick said. "If he's the same guy from about a hundred jobs and a handful of body modifications ago."

"You're not that old," Simone said.

"I've seen things," Rick replied. "Anyway, whether or not it's Mikey, that asshole *is* crazy. Impressively so. You know how it is in this world, all of us liars and worse. Still, I think he went by the Carver, then Choppy for a while after that. Both of those were during his knife phase. But Mikey or whoever eventually grew out of that."

He paused, waiting for either one of them to inquire about Mikey Carver Choppy's current interests as Salsa. They didn't, but no matter. Simone had unconsciously tipped her body forward in baited expectation, waiting to hear more about the assassin named Salsa. Embarrassingly, after a quick check, Emily realized she'd done the same.

Rick had them hooked on his every word, damn him.

He continued. "Salsa got his newest name because he takes a piece of each target home with him. Cuts 'em into tiny little pieces. Thin, like slivers of garlic. Then he mixes those pieces in with his homemade salsa and sends it to the victim's loved ones."

"Fuck," Emily said.

"How is that 'impressive'?" Simone asked.

"He has his own labels made, and I've heard the salsa's

out of this world. He clearly puts a lot of care into it. Uses some sort of habanero peppers, and pureed carrots for color. Most of us do the job and leave it behind us. Salsa takes his work home with him." Rick shrugged. "*Impressive.*"

"Well, even Salsa would probably be smart enough to stay away from the DEA's evidence room," Emily said.

"You're probably right, but I don't see Salsa as being the sort of fellow to see the end of this contest, despite his ethic. He's one hell of a butcher, but the man ain't no surgeon. You want to win this, or at least get the chance for a second round, I just gave you the answer."

"No, you didn't," Emily said. "You might as well have told us about a great idea for making money, then explained that Fort Knox has some gold."

"That's hardly the same." Rick rolled his eyes.

"It's an impossible task."

"Well, I don't see it that way."

Simone watched the two of them but stayed out of the argument.

"I'm not saying it'll be easy, but it's possible with the right plan."

"But you haven't even given us that plan!" Emily exclaimed.

"You haven't given me much of a chance, sun—"

"You've been talking for almost half an hour!"

Yet another shrug. "Good things come to those who wait. I was about to tell you all the details when y'all started calling me crazy. That last anecdote was on account of my needing to defend myself."

"Are you a child?" Emily asked.

He looked her up and down with a widening smirk. "Less than you."

"So, what we've learned here is that you're great at

buying time and telling us a bunch of bullshit but not in actually delivering anything of value. We're done here." Emily turned to Simone, assuming her partner would play along. "What should we do with him?"

"I want to hear his plan." Then Simone looked at Rick and narrowed her eyes. "What makes you so sure we can get in and out of the evidence room?"

"I never said I was sure," Rick corrected.

"Then how do you know it's *possible?*" Simone pressed.

Rick grinned. "Because I've done it before."

"He's lying," Emily said.

"We'll be back." Simone took Emily by the arm then led her to one of the apartment's two bedrooms.

After she closed the door, Emily shook her off. "Stop acting like you're my mother about to put me in a time out."

"I need you to start acting sensible," Simone said.

"Are you kidding me? You're the one who wants to play pat-a-cake with a criminal."

"I want to get answers. And right now, he has more than you do."

"Or so he promised," Emily argued. "But all I've seen so far is him trying to pass off a mission from Grand Theft Auto as a viable idea. Just so we're clear, it's not. We follow that idiot, and we're going to get ourselves killed."

"Are you forgetting what side we're on? We can abort whenever we want to. It makes a lot more sense to see where he's going with this, regardless of whether you think it's good or even possible. This is about discovery. And he's right that we'll lose it all if we do nothing."

"Do you really think he believes we can pull this off?" Emily asked. "Or is it possible he's only buying time? Again."

"Of course, it's possible, but I would have to ask *why*. If

I were him and trying to stall, I'd work at least a hundred other angles before I'd ever suggest breaking into the DEA's evidence room."

"So, you believe him *because* he's being ludicrous."

"What does he have to gain with a story like that?" Simone asked.

"Us going into another room to argue about it."

"What do we have to lose by going along with it?"

"We're breaking the law," Emily answered.

"Bullshit. We're doing our jobs. We can't do nothing. This mission is bigger than the law. Points will help us to advance in the contest. And even better, if we pull this off, Rick will trust us."

"Why do we even care?"

Simone said, "Because he knows something, and I want to know what. But more than that, he's camouflage. You saw it at the Gardens, people seem to know who he is. Our traveling in a pack gives us a little more legitimacy, and I'd argue we could use it."

"You want to use Rick to prove we're not undercover?"

"Among other things, yes."

Emily was hating the quickly developing habit, but yet again, as though she had no control over the script, and her life was going along according to words on a page she couldn't see, she begrudgingly agreed.

"Look on the bright side." Simone started walking back toward the bedroom door.

"There is one?"

"All that stalking you learned in Sniper School, I bet you're about to put it to use."

"Goodie."

Chapter Eight

THERE WASN'T much to Rick's plan, once it was finally all out of his mouth.

"You're a sniper, right?"

That's how Rick had started. After Emily agreed, he told them she just needed to use the same stealth approaching techniques she'd learned in Sniper School. He would hold down the fort while Emily and Simone tried to breech the building. He might as well have started with, *Simone was right.*

There wasn't much more to it than that, though it sure seemed like it with the amount of time it took him to spill it. By the final punchline the reason for his drawing it out became clearer. The entire plan was only possible because he knew a guy with access. They needed to reach a certain point by themselves, then Rick's contact could get them the rest of the way.

"Again," Emily said, "you just happen to have a contact."

"Not exactly. I have a contact who has a contact. He probably has a contact, too, but I stop caring after that second one. This is Miami. Everyone has someone in the DEA. Probably the same guy." Rick shook his head, now sounding irritated. "According to my math, y'all should be over the moon. I've more than done my part here, and I'll more than do it on the ground. You two ready for yours? How about it, sunshine?"

"Readier than you," she answered like a child.

Emily was as good on the ground as she was behind the scope. She hadn't exactly breezed through her training, but even her best instructors couldn't hide their surprise. Not the first time she should have blown her run, nor the last time after months of conditioning. Her father had prepared her as a little girl, both with makeshift courses at home and stories about what it took to get her head in the moment, then stay there.

Snipers had to move like a snake on a tree trunk and with the patience of a sloth. Beyond methodical. They might have to lie for days in the same position, observing, staying invisible. Snipers were a study in staying frozen. Thanks to her father, Emily knew the marvels of stalking long before her professional training. It was amazing the things people passed over on the ground. But when sneaking up on someone, an anthill looked like a mountain. Picking one position then crawling to the next, every move yet another bet on her life.

She asked the same questions every time.

Will that new spot cover me? And what's the safest way to get there?

The game she was playing now wasn't her first. Stalk training had been a game, as well, albeit with lesser stakes. Open grassy ranges. Students started at one end, a thousand meters down range. A pair of instructors sat atop a tower with spotter scopes. Students had to advance toward the instructors and stay invisible. Not just to the spotters, but to the walkers on the ground. Once in position, the student snipers took a shot. Really, they were looking through the scope to see what it said on the card they were holding, or how many fingers they were showing on their hands. Even firing blanks, students had to be careful. A muzzle flash or a kick of dirt was a tattletale to their position.

After the first shot, snipers stalked to their next spot and fired a second time. It was a pass-fail game. The snipers were out the second they were spotted. Too many fails and the student flunked out.

But that's not what happened to Emily.

"Have you already talked to your guy?" Simone asked.

"Of course not. I've been here with you lovely ladies."

Emily turned to him. "How do you know your guy can be there when we need him?"

"I don't. But it's probably a good start if I call him and ask."

They let him call. After two minutes of clearly coded conversation, he hung up. "We're good to go."

"What was all that bullshit you were saying?" Emily asked.

"I was setting things up, just like you asked." Rick gave her a smile.

"How do we know you didn't tell your guy to take us down when we get there?"

Still smiling, he said, "You don't. Is this protocol after every question now? Y'all asking me if I'm about to set you up? Here's a spoiler alert for this little adventure of ours. I will absolutely double-cross you at some point. That's the game we're playing, and you'd be a fool to believe otherwise. But you'd also be an idiot's cousin if you think I'd do something stupid a second before it serves me to do so. And right now, it's in my best or at least better interests to secure the confiscated shipment. And hopefully the cash, if there was another leak in the yard. The two of you are a part of that plan."

"When are we going, then?" Simone asked.

"We'd be on our way already if I wasn't required to explain it all over again."

Rick was omnipresent after that. Even when they went to the bathroom before leaving it was one at a time, so Simone and Emily couldn't decompress. But it wasn't hard to imagine what her handler was thinking. They had to be sharing similar thoughts. This felt like a setup. Probably was. But there wasn't much of a choice. They could either go along with Rick and see where it took them or fail the mission entirely. That was unacceptable to Emily, and for sure Simone would agree.

They drove in silence. Parked in the shadows. Approached the building like roaches.

Rick stayed with the car, calling out orders for where to go and what to avoid. Emily wanted to kill him. Half of what he said sounded like he was fucking with them. The other half, she was certain he was.

"Wait," he would call out. "Stay back. There's a pigtailed girl with a lollipop rounding the corner. Hold on … yeah, her T-shirt says, *Surely not everyone was kung-fu fighting.*"

"Asshole," Simone muttered.

"Exactly," Emily agreed.

"I can hear you."

"Then mission accomplished," Simone said.

Rick was back in their ears. "In all seriousness, you're about to see a fucker you're gonna wanna kill."

Neither of them bothered to correct him. He was probably just trying to get under their skin. They'd discussed it repeatedly. No unnecessary casualties. Stolen evidence was one thing, but murder to set off a manhunt was something else entirely. Their resistance wasn't even suspicious. You didn't have to work for the United States Government to know Rick was being reckless if not next level ridiculous.

The "fucker they were gonna wanna kill" walked right by them.

Emily was closer, completely covered in shadows. Simone nodded to her, Emily nodded back, then she slipped out of her nook and into the night like she was a part of it. Jumped on the man's back and had two fingers to his throat before her legs were circling his waist.

He spilled to the ground, then Simone emerged from the shadows to help her drag his body into the darkness.

"You should be good for a while now. Don't go past the red door. That's where MacDonald will meet you."

"Is that his real name?" Emily asked.

"Of course not," Rick answered.

Even after the red door was visible in the distance, it took them a while to crawl there. Rick kept making crass jokes, though Emily didn't understand why he would want to. He shouldn't be trying to make them laugh aloud. And if he knew his jokes weren't funny, then he was being intentionally annoying while they were trying to work. Either way, what an asshole.

"Why didn't the astronaut come home to his wife?" Of course, they both ignored him, and of course, Rick delivered the punchline himself. "Because he needed his space."

They were finally in front of the red door, as close as the tangle of shadows could get them.

"Wait there," Rick said, his voice suddenly moving from mischievous to serious. "MacDonald will be out in a minute."

But Simone pushed back. "We're not waiting out here. There's no cover. We're going back. He can meet—"

"I said stay there," Rick barked. "He'll be out in a second."

They stood in the light, fully exposed, Simone tapping her foot. "We need to get out of here."

"No shit," Emily said.

Another several seconds passed, then Simone decided she couldn't take it anymore and slipped back into the shadows.

"You're just going to leave me here by myself?" Emily whisper-shouted into the darkness.

"You're welcome to join me," Simone whisper-shouted back.

Emily turned her back on the shadows and looked at the red door. She took another step toward it, studying something in a cluster of shadows on the other side of Simone's hiding spot. She stood upright, spun toward Simone. "I think—"

But then hands were on Emily, dragging her back as she screamed.

There was a flash of movement, then Simone darted from the shadows.

She raised her gun as she came, and for a moment Emily imagined Simone had forgotten her side of the law, but then she brought the butt of her weapon down hard on the attacker's head. His grip on Emily relaxed, and he slumped down to the ground.

The red door swung open. On the other side stood a tall man with a giant mustache. He didn't have overalls or anything else that would paint this particular picture, and it was also possible it was merely the power of suggestion, but Emily thought the man looked like a farmer the second she saw him.

"You must be MacDonald," Emily said.

"Who?" the man said.

Simone took the ball. "Rick sent us."

"I know Rick sent you," said MacDonald, obviously bothered. "Follow me."

He opened the red door, led them through a long maze of corridors that felt like it must have crossed into a second building, down one flight of stairs, through another long hallway, then up a separate flight. They finally stopped at room 2F.

"I can't stay with you," MacDonald said. "But what you need is in there, so have at it and be careful."

Simone thanked the man, then he left them alone to search for their prize.

They slipped inside. Emily tensed for an alarm to ring when the door opened, but they were greeted with nothing but quiet.

Didn't mean they didn't trip a silent alarm.

"This doesn't feel like a setup to you?" Emily asked, one eye on all the shelves full of evidence, the other scanning for hidden dangers.

"I'm not sure how many times you want me to answer that, but I'll try once more. Yes, this feels like a setup, and yes, everything about this feels off. Still, as we've amply covered, we don't really have much of a choice."

Emily didn't answer. She started looking faster as she moved through the evidence room alongside Simone. Fortunately, one of them understood how things were catalogued. But it wasn't Emily. She grew increasingly frustrated the longer she searched, while Simone seemed to be growing increasingly excited, her breath getting ever more shallow until she finally announced, "I found it!"

Emily ran over, and sure as shit, there it was. Not just their score, but more of it than either one of them had imagined or discussed. And Rick got his wish because the money was also there. The Coast Guard and DEA must have somehow hit both sides of the transaction.

A massive haul. And with only the three of them, they couldn't possibly take everything.

Rick's voice in their ears: "How are we doing in there?"

"There's a lot here," Simone said. "Too much."

"Sounds like a quality problem," Rick said. "I'll bring the car around."

"It's more than can fit in the car," Emily argued.

"Get what you can. I'll be right there."

"Maybe it's fine," Emily said. "We don't want the Outfit to have the money or the drugs. We're just trying to get points, and we can earn those regardless of what we actually leave with. Probably."

"Maybe." But Simone didn't sound like she believed it.

They loaded up as much as they could in some available duffel bags. Emily wanted to carry the money, but Simone saddled her with the drugs. They made their way back the way they came, two bags each, and were on the other side of the red door before alarms began to bray.

Who ratted them out? Rick? MacDonald? The guy Simone felled? Was there a silent alarm?

Didn't matter anymore. The damage was done.

They ran. No clear direction, just away from the building since they didn't see Rick anywhere.

"No warning ..." Emily panted as they ran. "Do you think he set us up?"

Simone looked at her but kept running without saying a word.

Chaos rained on the building as they raced away from it as fast as they could. An SUV pulled in front of them, its bright lights an assault.

"Keep running!" Simone yelled, veering away from Emily so the SUV might chase her. "I'll draw its attention."

She ran, and for a moment Emily even believed that she might escape the situation.

But she was grabbed from behind then yanked to the ground.

Chapter Nine

EMILY WASN'T IN PRISON. But she was a prisoner, nonetheless.

She wasn't even sure how many people had taken her down. She had felt the riot of limbs around her body dragging her to the ground before her arms were restrained. Then she was led into the locked room where she now waited for someone to come in or for something to happen.

Long term, Emily was surely fine. She had been doing her job, despite what it might have looked like to the good folks working this branch of the DEA. An armed thief in their midst — they were probably all in a meeting, determining what to do with her, who they should hand her off to. Checking jurisdiction, arguing custody. Anything and everything else. But she couldn't say a word to help herself because she couldn't afford to blow her cover.

It wasn't like admitting to being on a mission would make her problems magically go away. They would have to investigate her claims. That process wouldn't be straightforward or fast. In the meantime, MacDonald — or whatever his name was — would know the truth, along with any other potential leaks in the department.

Even if Emily managed to get out of trouble for breaking the law, she would have failed in her mission and her work with RICO would be finished.

Rick didn't warn them when he could have, not through MacDonald or into her ear. Plenty of jokes, though. And the miscreant sure did seem to be enjoying his perch away from the action. He was dirty by nature, so it made sense he would set her up. This was Emily's fault for being stupid enough to believe him.

Simone was a much harder puzzle to solve.

Her handler had managed to slip away while she got tackled then locked in this room. Dumb luck or by design? Emily could understand why Rick would want to set her up and get her out of the contest, but Simone's motives, if this was another betrayal, weren't nearly as clear. At least not yet. Seemed to Emily she was worth more in the game at this point than out of it. They weren't even out of round one.

Emily was still sitting in the chair where she had been shoved after getting dragged into this room. She wasn't restrained, but there was nothing to do. She combed the room for cameras but found none in any of the obvious places. Perhaps there were some too tiny to see or camouflaged in the wall. Not that it mattered. What could the cameras possibly be recording ... Emily thinking too hard?

The room was empty except for a half-dozen plastic chairs, one of them occupied.

There was a way out of this. And Emily was going to find it. And make her father proud.

The door swung open. MacDonald entered.

Her heart stopped for a second. In that moment, Emily

didn't know if she should be filled with fear or relief. As he approached, she grew swollen with both.

MacDonald dragged a seat over to Emily, positioned it too close to her body, then plopped down with a grunt preceding a sigh. He leaned forward, even closer, and said, "Now what are we going to do with you?"

To compensate for his proximity, Emily scooted her chair back then sat straighter. "You're with Rick."

He smiled. Bright white teeth like a highlight on his artifice. "Who?"

"The guy who calls you MacDonald."

"My name is Agent Jonathan Collins, and I have no idea what you're talking about." And still, the grin.

"I'm sure you're not the only person I'll be talking to around here, and I'm sure whoever else I speak with will be very interested to know it was you who let us into the evidence room."

"You're right." Collins scooted his chair another inch forward. "I'm sure they would enjoy your story. You, describing how a decorated agent opened the door for a couple of criminals ... the same agent who came in to question you face-to-face. I think we're probably better off if we do things my way instead."

"You're right. It's a ridiculous story. They'll see right through it. I'll just wait for my call."

Collins nodded in approval. "Smart. I could really see that working out for you. I'll check back with you tomorrow and see if you still want to wait."

"You can't do that. I have rights."

"A shit ton," Collins agreed. "It's annoying how many you have. But they don't mean dick while you're in here. You can raise a stink later, but seeing as you broke into a DEA evidence locker, I—"

"You let us in!"

"Enough with the fairytales, Rapunzel. This—"

"You're right, Agent Jonathan Collins, I can't prove you're a lying sack of shit. But I don't need to. Eventually, I'll get out of here. Unless you're planning to kill me. And I'm sure you would, if I wasn't in a DEA facility right now. But that's a reality you have to deal with. At some point, I'll get to make a call. You decide who I reach out to."

Emily paused. When Collins said nothing, she added, "Aren't you going to ask about my choices?"

He grunted, chewing on his bottom lip.

"I'll skip to the second choice since you didn't ask. You know Rick, so you also know what he does for a living. Off the record, of course. In case this is new information, I'm in the same line of work. The first thing I'll do when I get out of here is find out everything about you. Then, for free, I'll do what usually costs a fortune, and while wearing a smile that'll stick to my face for days. And if I don't get out of here, say I'm locked up for the rest of my life, I'll have one of my friends do it for me."

Still, he chewed his lip.

"But there's always my first choice."

"You wanna make a call? *Here.*"

Collins reached into his pocket, pulled out his phone, then handed it over to Emily like a grudge.

She dialed Tepper's number then waited four rings before she heard an error message informing her that the number had been disconnected. After a skip in her heart, she tried again, watching every number on the screen as she carefully pressed the digits.

The same error sounded.

Collins continued to stare.

Emily was sure the number was right. She had memorized it the same as she memorized most things, repeating it over and over to herself until she heard it as a song. That melody was looping in her mind right now, but her notes were apparently off.

Or worse. The entire operation could be a sham. Emily was the one locked in a room after breaking the law. Maybe she was getting set up for something much bigger than she'd originally suspected and had walked right into it.

The conspiracy was more than Simone. It was Tepper, too.

Emily had to find her breath. For a moment, it felt like her heart might collapse. If Tepper was at the top of this subterfuge, then more than Emily's career was at stake. Her freedom might be in jeopardy, too.

She tried once more. Tepper's number was still disconnected.

"Trouble on the line?" Collins asked.

She tried Simone, but that went straight to voicemail as well. At least that number appeared to remain viable.

Emily dialed Rick next, but of course he didn't answer. And his outgoing message pissed her off.

"Yo yo yo, it's Rick. So, funny story ... my phone and I are playing hide 'n seek, and wouldn't you know it, the fucker is winning. I'll call you back when I find it. If I have a good reason to. But let's be real, this is probably a fuck you."

Probably? She thought not. It was definitely a fuck-you, right in her face.

"I think that's enough." Collin opened his palm, presumably waiting for his phone.

Emily handed it over. "I want to see a lawyer."

Collin nodded with understanding. "I want to see if my girlfriend will blow me in the back of a theater, but so far it's been a no-go, even after I bought her a nice sweater before our movie the last time."

"Charming."

"She says it's not a fair expectation because she misses part of the movie."

"Is there a reason you're in here?" Emily asked. "I mean, officially."

"I just thought you and I should have a chat, before things got 'official.' Someone else will be in here soon, and I didn't want you saying anything unnecessarily foolish for us both. Now that I'm questioning you, your description of the man who led you to the evidence room means about as much as a bag of magic beans. You will go down for this, but we both know someone like you has a lot of legal resources. You'll be out on bail in no time, then I'm sure you'll disappear. Both of us don't need to go down."

"Sounds fair," Emily said.

Collins stood. "Don't make this harder on yourself. Help me help you."

"Got it — protect the asshole at all costs."

He turned back at the door. "I'm sure you'll do the right thing."

And then he was gone.

Fuck. Emily would have pounded her fist through the wall if her trigger finger wasn't a treasure.

But still, every minute felt excruciating. She sat in the chair with her eyes closed, trying to piece the puzzle together. It all seemed off, and nothing quite fit. Only when—

She opened her eyes at the sound of the door unlocking.

As it swung open, Emily readied herself for Collins. Or worse.

But it was Simone. "Let's get out of here."

Emily was up and out of her seat, a beat behind Simone as they ran.

No questions as she followed. No stealth maneuvers as

they fled the facility. Simone seemed to know exactly where she was going, so Emily stayed right behind her, feet pounding on the ground, her heart like a tympani.

"We're here." Simone slowed to a walk in front of an old Toyota Tacoma parked a few blocks away. She opened the driver's door, got inside, then unlocked the passenger side.

The engine was already on as Emily climbed. Simone tore into the street before her door was even closed.

"So, that happened," she said.

"What exactly is *that*?" Emily asked.

"I just busted you out of a DEA facility."

"And exactly how did you do that?"

"I bribed a guard. It was easy enough with all that cash."

"Great," Emily said. "Another law broken."

"You've *got* to be kidding me!" Simone slammed her hand on the dashboard.

"We're in yet another stolen car, right? Don't get me wrong, I'm grateful for the rescue, but I've lost count of how many crimes you've committed since we started this mission. Murder, evidence theft, bribery — all before *breaking me out of jail*."

"So ... I should have left you in there? And weren't you with me on that stolen boat?"

"Yes, I was. Because you made me—"

"I didn't *make you* do anything, Emily. You stole a boat, you broke into an evidence holding facility, and you broke out of jail."

"This wasn't what I signed up for."

"I think this is exactly what you signed up for," Simone said. I'm just not who you wanted to do this with." She fumed in silence for a few seconds, nostrils flaring as she fought to control her ragged breaths. "Emily, this has become a problem. Bigger than I envisioned and bigger than I can overcome without you changing your attitude."

"Do enlighten me." She crossed her arms.

"You don't know how to grow up and face the reality that life isn't as black and white as you've always seen it."

"We are who we spend our time with. It's better to be alone than in bad company. My dad used to say that."

"So, you've told me."

"Sorry for boring you," Emily said.

"Your father's passing has clouded your entire world perspective. You can't see things for what they are because you're too busy seeing them for some idealized way of how you want them to be."

"Thanks, doc. Please pass the Prozac."

"You'll be one of the best when you—"

"This isn't what I signed up for."

"Emily—"

"I want out. You can—"

"Damn it. Will you shut up and listen for one hot minute? You need to see the bigger picture. Quitting now leaves you without a career. But seeing this through to the end? Not only will you save countless lives if we manage to bring the Outfit down, you'll be set up for any job you want. Consider our respective ages and experience, or lack thereof. Neither of us deserve this chance yet, and both of us know it. This is as big as it gets."

Resentment bubbled inside Emily, honor grating against her intentions.

Her dad would want her to see the bigger picture. To be a hero like he was.

"What do you suggest we do?" Emily asked.

"Get back in the contest and see where it goes."

"How are we going to do that? What are we waiting for?"

Simone's phone rattled against the sides of the center console as it buzzed. She picked it up, glanced from the road to the screen for two seconds, then looked back through the windshield.

Without explanation, she turned the Tacoma around.

Chapter Ten

"What is it?" Emily asked. "Where are we going."

"The next location. Everyone is supposed to meet in an hour."

"What if we were more than an hour away?"

"Then tough shit," Simone said. "The winners wouldn't be. They'd be somewhere near the shipment."

"It's almost one in the morning. What if they were sleeping … or in a strip club with the—"

"Then they would miss the call and deserve to fail. The Foreman is looking for the best."

Their car on the road was the only sound after that. Until Simone broke the silence. "I'm not saying you should work for the Foreman—"

"Work for the Foreman! He's a crime lord!"

"I meant if we get through all the trials. What I mean is — and mind you, I don't think you're there yet — but you could be the best, you know. If you could just get over a few things."

"Like honor and integrity?"

"Like getting fixed in a single world view—"

"Character and honesty."

"—so you can't see anything outside of the—"

"Virtue and decency."

"—way you've always seen it, and oh my God, are you finished?" She sighed. "I get why you joined military, Emily. This is legacy for you, it isn't for me."

Again, there was silence.

But this time Emily broke it. "Why did you join the military?"

She didn't know the story. Not really. Not all of it. Simone had always asked a lot of questions. Emily loved to talk about her father, so answering was easy. Asking that question now, she realized how rarely she had bounced the ball back. And how little Simone had ever volunteered.

"You know why," Simone said.

"I only know the stuff we've talked about a few times. You grew up poor, so the Army was an escape. Your grades were shit and your parents are assholes. That made you kind of an asshole, too."

"Wow. That's an excellent summary. I should change my LiveLyfe profile."

Emily laughed. "Did I get anything wrong?"

"I think you've missed some of the nuance." But Simone laughed, too. "Bottom line, you entered the military to honor your father. I saw it as my only choice. That's framed how each of us has seen everything. It's like your whole 'we are who we spend our time with' thing."

"It's true."

"Sure, it's true," Simone agreed. "But there are a lot of truths. You act like that's the only one, or at least the only one that matters."

Another silence followed that, but this one was heavier than the last few had been.

Simone tried to improve it. "Do you have a picture of

your dad? All those stories you've told, and I've never seen him."

Emily laughed uncomfortably. "You don't really want to see him."

"Sure, I do. Why wouldn't I?"

"What difference does it make? He's just another face."

"You're infuriating sometimes, you know that?" Simone looked at Emily, waited for her to acknowledge her admonishing stare, then turned her attention back to the road. "He's not 'just another face.' This is someone I've heard a lot of stories about. When I'm reading a book and it's talking about a real person, I run a Forage search to see what they look like. You saw how many photos I've memorized! It's what I do."

"Then why haven't you ever asked before?"

"Because you're touchy when it comes to your father. I didn't want to overstep."

"And now?" Emily asked.

"Now we need to get over that shit."

Emily laughed again, her most involuntary chuckle so far. She took out her wallet, pulled out her father's picture, then offered it to Simone.

With one hand still on the wheel, Simone took the picture, then traded her attention between it and the road, back and forth for long enough that it was feeling dangerous by the time she finally handed it back.

"What is it?" Emily asked, unnerved by Simone's expression.

"I don't know. Probably nothing."

"It's something."

No response.

"What is it, Simone?"

"He looks familiar. But I can't place how."

"How can he look familiar?"

"Do you have any uncles?"

"Not that I know of," Emily said. "He probably has one of those faces."

"Maybe." Then nothing.

Emily wasn't sure how to tiptoe around that, and her change in topic was a gamble, but she rolled the dice anyway. "What about your dad? Do you have a picture of him?"

"Hell no," Simone said. "If you find one, hand it over so I can light that shit on fire. You lost your dad early. I wish I'd lost mine."

"You don't mean that."

"I absolutely, truly do."

"Why?" Emily asked.

"Because he was responsible for everything terrible that happened to me before I finally got control over my own life. I think he left home when I was three, though I've never gotten a straight answer and can't remember back that far. I know my mom drove him away because she was a monster when she drank, which was all the time. He couldn't stand her, but she was still good enough for his daughter. So, he left us both. She started using. I saw him after that. Sometimes a lot. But he got worse and worse over time and only came over to drink or have sex with my mom. I was too young to understand and had to piece most of it together later on my own. But I would hear the mattress squeaking and the sounds of slapping and ..."

Simone stopped. She didn't need to continue, and Emily had more than she needed. Her life hadn't been amazing by a long shot, but it was leaps and bounds better than Simone's. She had the world's best father before his death, and her mom started loving Emily twice as hard in the wake of his passing.

"I'm sorry," Emily said.

"You don't need to be."

Silence returned, but this time it felt like a blanket instead of a pall.

A quarter hour later, they pulled up to the address with ten minutes left on the clock. They were at a warehouse with a large yard, fenced off and vacant of cars. The empty lot was likely necessary to maintain the illusion that nothing was happening here. The neighboring few blocks were private property and tow away zones. By the time they found a space, they had only five minutes left and at least that long a walk before they made it back to the warehouse.

"Are you sure we should be parking here?" Emily asked, looking around at all the broken glass and flickering lights.

"Do we have a choice?"

"There's at least an eighty-percent chance our tires will be gone by the time we get back, right?"

Simone ignored her. She broke into a light jog as she crossed the first street with barely a glance.

Emily scurried after her.

They cut it close.

The warehouse was settling into a quiet as they slipped inside. A barrel-chested bouncer nodded at them as they entered then locked the door behind them. Emily spied Jackie-O and Arcade as the duo found their place in the back.

Amil nodded with a smile to greet them as his gaze swept across the crowd.

He gave it a second sweep, but this time, his smile faded. By the third pass, he was raking his glare across the assembled killers.

Emily's blood chilled as her thermostat of danger cranked hard to the right.

"The Forman is most displeased with the results of our first trial. This is beyond a mild annoyance." Amil began to pace. "I've never seen him so vexed. The man is downright needled. It was a grand idea, assembling the best of you. But in execution, the endeavor has proven itself to be a disappointment. This first experiment has been a massive failure. A shipment was lost to the Coast Guard and handed over to the DEA. The cash has been confiscated. Our enemies and competitors should be trembling in fear because they are being outmaneuvered, not shaking their fists at the incompetence derailing their pipeline."

Amil paused for a painfully long eon of half a minute or so, letting the assembled assassins stew in his words. He continued to pace the stage, still raking his gaze across the crowd until he finally stopped in the middle. "Does anyone here have something to say?"

"Turns out, someone does."

The crowd parted for the speaker — Rick.

He made his way toward the stage, holding a big black duffel in each hand. He set both bags on the stage, looked up at Amil, out at the crowd with a shit-eating grin, then back up at his host. "It ain't nowhere near the whole haul, but I bet my big swinging sack and all the seed in it that it's at least a billion times more than anyone here's got, since even infinity times zero is still zero."

Amil bent down to the bags, unzipped each in turn, peered inside, then nodded at Rick without any expression. Amil leaned forward, whispered in his ear, then walked away. Rick followed him to the edge of the stage where the two of them quietly conferred.

It was a long, private discussion.

"What do you think they're talking about?" Simone whispered.

"About what's next. Or maybe how to change the game, since he's the only one who can advance."

"You don't know that. Rick's the only one with a haul, but other points could have been earned that we don't know about."

"Maybe Salsa sent the Foreman a jar of someone special," Emily said.

"That's not funny. I want to know how Rick ended up with the drugs, and with the money, which I gave to the guard."

"Probably Collins."

"Who?" Simone asked.

"MacDonald."

Amil called the room to order, not that anyone was out of it.

"Will Demize and BullZi please come to the front?"

Emily swallowed then walked to the front alongside Simone.

When they got there, Amil said, "Meteor has informed me he had some help in recovering what belonged to the Outfit."

Simone and Emily traded a look, both of them surely thinking *WTF?* and *METEOR?*

Not that their names were much better.

Amil looked down at them then out at the crowd. "Meteor has passed this round in first place with a total of fifty points. Demize and BullZi are now tied for second place with a total of twenty-five points each. The rest of you, unfortunately, are a disgrace. The Outfit, however, is still hunting for the best, so you will be given another chance. Each of you has an opportunity to prove you aren't pathetic and put these first three into last place where they belong."

After a few more not-so-encouraging words, Amil

revealed their next target. A launderer named Asher, vacationing in a private villa in Palm Beach. He would be having a party the following night.

"Inside his safe is a Zip drive containing a full list of his clients and all their transactions. The Foreman cares *only about the Zip drive*. Anything else is yours to keep. However, if additional loot will in any way prevent you from delivering the drive, he strongly suggests you leave it be and revel in the rewards that will be coming as winner of this contest. The Foreman would also like you to understand that while it isn't a necessary part of finishing this mission, there will be additional points awarded for eliminating the launderer himself."

Amil looked out at the audience, offered them a barely supplicant bow, then said, "We wish you luck."

He wasn't even off of the stage before Simone was pulling Emily back through the crowd.

"Where are we going?"

"Somewhere to sleep," Simone said.

That might be the world's best idea, but still ... "Shouldn't we say thank you to Rick?"

They were already outside the warehouse. Simone was walking fast for how tired she had to be. Emily could barely keep up.

"No, we shouldn't say *thank you* to Rick! Fuck Rick."

"We wouldn't be in second and third place if it wasn't for him," Emily argued.

"Or maybe we would have handed Amil the drugs and cash ourselves."

She was already on the other side of the fence and still walking fast toward their stolen truck.

"Shouldn't we—"

"No," Simone cut her off. "We shouldn't. Under no

circumstances does Rick or Meteor or whoever he is deserve the benefit of your doubt. Or mine."

There were no further arguments the rest of their way to the Tacoma.

"FUCK!" Simone cried out, still a few steps ahead of Emily.

"Are the tires gone?"

"Close." Simone pointed.

Emily followed her finger to the Tacoma's tires. The two she saw were slashed, and judging by the truck's position on the ground, there was a matching set on the other side.

"Looks like maybe it's time to go ahead and say thank you to Meteor."

Chapter Eleven

"Slow down!" Simone called behind her.

Emily yelled without slowing or turning around. "Are you kidding me? You sure were in a hurry a few minutes ago."

"I was *walking*. You're running."

Still running, Emily spoke through her exhales. "We have to hurry, or we're going to miss our ride."

There was no use arguing, so they shut their mouths and ran harder.

Two minutes later, they were back at the warehouse, inside the fence, working to catch their breath so they could accidentally run back into Rick.

It didn't take long, so they were still out of breath. He came over while Emily was still huffing.

"I was hoping I'd run into y'all before splitting. Even hung around a few minutes extra in case I saw you. Good thing since it looks like I did." He grinned.

"What were you hoping would happen if you found us?" Simone asked with too much edge in her voice.

"A thank you might be nice."

Simone glared at him. "You execute people for a living, and you need us to say *thank you?*"

"Credit where credit was due."

"We were hoping you might want to carpool," Emily said.

Rick turned to her. "*We* or *you?*"

"We." After a pause, she added, "Mostly me."

Rick seemed to consider, then he nodded thoughtfully before tipping his chin at Simone. "Seeing as this one killed my last wingman, I suppose I could use some extra hands, especially seeing as this pair owes me."

"We don't owe you," Simone said.

He flashed another grin. "If you say so."

"When are we going?" Emily asked.

"Five minutes." Rick raised his right hand, palm out. "I promised Garfield I'd say goodbye."

"We can't do this," Simone said the second Rick was out of earshot.

"Get a ride? You would rather steal another car?"

"Of course, I'd rather steal another car. That man is clearly a psychopath. I don't think we should be anywhere around him."

"You mean keeping an eye on him? That seems like exactly what we should be doing."

"Why *him?*" Simone asked.

"Because we're supposed to be getting closer to the Outfit, and he's the only one we have an in with. Not to mention, he's in first place. His standing has to be pretty good."

"We're in second."

"Thanks to him."

Simone flung her hands in the air. "You're not uncomfortable with his blasé attitude toward murder?"

"Of course, I am!" Emily was too loud, so she lowered

her voice. "But we need a ride, and there's more benefit here than cost."

"I'm not sure I agree." Simone shook her head. "This is a bad idea."

"Well, I don't see much of a choice."

They had to stop, and even pretended to smile, as Rick approached.

"Things all sewn up with Garfield?" Simone asked.

"Air tight. Now, let's ramble." Rick turned around then started walking toward an alternate exit, across the yard and through another door in the fence. "VIP parking," he explained while holding it open for them.

He had changed cars. Upgraded to a matte black Range Rover, clearly some sort of special edition. Emily felt uncomfortable getting in, but she did. Even after Rick insisted on her riding shotgun. It was definitely better than the lowrider.

"Anyone have a musical preference?" he asked after starting the engine.

"Whatever you want," Emily said.

"Whichever artist keeps you from talking," added Simone.

"Any objection to Billy Joel?"

Billy Joel?

"Don't look at me like that, sunshine. Billy don't get half the credit he deserves. People are always like, fuck 'Uptown Girl,' but fuck them right back in the face. Billy Joel sold out Madison Square Garden more times than anyone in history, and he played to fifty thousand people at Dodger Stadium."

"Super impressive," Simone said, "and highly relevant to our lives right now."

Rick looked down at his phone, scrolled for a few moments, then set it into the center console. He pulled into the street as Billy Joel's 'Pressure' pounded through the speakers.

"I'm just saying," Rick continued like either she or Simone cared, "Billy should get more respect. Everyone's always slobbering all over Elton John, but Bernie writes everything for him."

"He's probably never heard that before," Simone chimed in from the back, though it was the last thing she said for a while.

Emily ended up falling into an actual conversation with Rick about the line between commercial and being great.

"'She's Always a Woman' is both!" He punched the steering wheel.

Emily was grateful for the rapport she had managed to establish with Rick over such a relatively short period of time. It made conversation easier during their ride along the coast. But even better, she had solved a problem. Because of her, they now had a ride to the next target. And placement in the contest. Thanks to her, they were closer to the inside.

To her way of thinking, that was more than pulling her own weight.

And she controlled this relationship. Emily was up front, and Rick was talking to *her*, while Simone sat in the back. It felt silken on her skin, and for at least a while from up there in front, Emily wanted to enjoy it.

"So, Meteor, huh?" Emily laughed.

"Ain't nothing wrong with that. Strikes me as one of the better names in circulation. A meteor is the most dangerous object known to humanity, and don't even get me started on your moniker."

Emily laughed again, then she slapped the dashboard. "This is nice. Was it at the safe house? I wish I'd gotten this instead of that old Cadillac."

Without looking over he said, "I had to relieve a young man of his life for this one. But I can promise you, that kid did not appreciate what he had."

"I can't tell if you're kidding." Emily could feel Simone staring daggers into the back of her head.

"It wasn't indiscriminate," Rick explained. "I hid in the backseat like I usually do, so I can make an informed decision. I didn't even need five minutes. The guy called not one but two different girls he's fucking, before calling his wife and telling his baby daughter how much he loved her. I also think he was stealing from work, but that's just a hunch."

"You murder people for a living!" Emily exclaimed.

"That's not an accurate statement. I don't have to work, as my family has plenty. I just appreciate living a life of purpose."

That wasn't a statement Emily could respond to, so she let the words marinate in silence and tried to ignore Simone's intensity behind her.

"Do you think your life has purpose now?" her handler finally asked from the back.

"Damn right it has purpose."

"How so?" Emily dared.

"I ain't eliminating any of the good people in this world, that's for damn sure. I take out the garbage. You can think that's rationalizing, and I ain't gonna argue with it because I know what it looks like to explain away your misbehaviors. But that's not what I'm doing here." Rick shook his head, adamant. "That human waste didn't deserve to drive a car like this. Or the wife he was cheating on. Fuck him. Same asshole, different suit and day job. The dickhead still deserves to die."

"And you don't?" Simone asked.

"Course I do." Rick turned around to glare at her.

"Rick ..." Emily prompted, after he'd had it turned for too long.

He slowly returned his gaze to the road.

After a minute of listening to their tires eating road, Emily said, "Is there a reason you seem to hate everyone so much?"

"I don't hate everyone. Just myself half the time and everyone else most of the rest of it."

"But why?" Emily pressed.

"Because people are shit."

"You weren't born thinking that way, so what makes you think people are shit now?"

"They are," he told Emily. "They lie and steal and gamble and cheat and kill. There's no use playing by the rules because everyone is breaking them, we're just all doing it to different degrees. So, if I'm gonna do something, why not do it better than anyone else?"

"You mean killing?" Emily confirmed.

"I mean living."

"Are you trying to prove something?" She continued to push him.

"Of course not. But that don't mean I won't."

"And who will you prove it to?"

"No one, like I said, but I'll be glad when my father can see that I can do anything. It's not that my dad doubts what I'm capable of so much as he's used to me doing it, so it doesn't register anymore."

"So, he doesn't really see you," Emily said. "It's the same way with my mom."

Rick turned from the road to give her a smile then went right back to staring through the windshield.

Emily had another daring question, but this one felt like a deeper level of peril. She imagined him flying off the handle. She had seen Rick's anger before, and the way it edged the irrational. She didn't want to be stuck in a car with him while he lost his shit. He might drive them all into a tree. Or a crowd of people.

But she listened to his breathing for more than a minute before deciding he was calm enough and her question was worth the risk.

"Do you think your dad would be proud if he knew you were a criminal?"

Rick started to laugh, almost hysterically.

Emily looked at him, then stole a glance at a baffled Simone.

"What is it?" Emily asked. "What's so funny?"

"Yes. My father puts more stock in doing something well than he does in the particulars of whatever that thing is," Rick explained, his smile still there. "In other words, I have no doubt my dad wouldn't give the wettest of shits if I worked for a crime syndicate, so long as I was one of the assholes in charge."

"How could your father not care?"

Rick turned to Emily with a smirk. "Have I told you what my father does for a living?"

"You said your family owns a chain of furniture stores called Kathmandu."

He looked back at the road and Emily exhaled. She stole another glance at Simone before facing front.

"That's right," Rick said. "And what do you think our business is?"

"You sell furniture. Knick-knacks. The shit they sell at Pier One."

"A front. A ruse. We launder money. It's simple. We buy some piece of crap from some place in the middle of nowhere for like ten cents a unit, then we sell it for like two-hundred bucks and lie about most of the particulars. It's more complicated than that, but there you go for the most part. So no, sunshine, I don't think my old man would object to my working with criminals. Knowing the fucker like I do, he'd probably pat himself on the back for teaching me right."

She longed to get out of the car, but they still had an hour of driving. Emily had been raised under the shadow cast by her father, a true hero, and couldn't fathom a collapse in morals such as the one Rick was showing her, abandoning all hope in humanity to embrace an empty and withered philosophy.

Rick and Simone didn't benefit from having a father whose example was a beacon in the darkness. But that didn't mean Emily would let their prejudices blacken her soul. She could see this through, do her job, and all without crossing that ever-shifting line her two companions constantly ignored, often with delight.

Rick was a sociopath.

Simone was an opportunist.

Emily was the only righteous one in the car.

Her present company was less than ideal. Even so, she would make her father proud.

Even if it killed her.

Chapter Twelve

Pickings were slim by the time they arrived in Palm Beach the following day.

Places close to Asher's villa were expensive, and while that wasn't a problem for Rick — apparently thanks to his family's lucrative laundering business — Emily and Simone had to watch their expenses. They played it off as though it were nothing, sharing a room because they wanted to and not because they had no other choice. Rick was sleeping several floors above them. They agreed to meet in the lobby for recon and strategizing before the big event then grumbled their goodbyes.

"Something crawl up your ass?" Emily asked Simone as they stepped off the elevator, leaving Rick to ride alone the rest of the way while they walked to their room.

"I'm tired."

"And pissed about something."

"I'm not pissed, though it is exhausting to hear you debate ethics for hours with an admitted criminal." Then Simone added, "Or more like *gleeful*."

"We're here, aren't we?"

"We could have made it here by ourselves."

"Right, supposing we were willing to steal yet another vehicle."

Simone rolled her eyes as she swiped her keycard. After the lock released, she opened the door, waited for Emily to enter, stepped inside, then closed the door behind them.

There was no wind-down. They each went to the bathroom, but neither took showers, brushed teeth, or bothered with miscellaneous grooming. While Simone used the toilet, Emily plugged in her phone, and after Emily left the restroom a few minutes later, it looked like Simone was already sleeping.

Before she flipped off the light, she glanced at her wallet on the shared nightstand between the beds. Might be the lack of sleep, but she swore it wasn't where she'd left it.

Emily pulled it to her side of the table and nudged it until it was perfectly aligned with the corner.

She was tempted to ask Simone if she'd moved it, but there was no point in waking her. Especially since Emily had no money for her to steal.

Instead, she put it out of her mind, slipped between the sheets, closed her eyes. Sleep claimed her immediately.

The night was gone in a blink. They hadn't closed the drapes, so Emily woke to gallons of bright light as it poured into their room. Simone was already up, pacing their small space. She glanced over at Emily, seeming half-surprised to see her eyes opened. The other half seemed reassured, maybe even pleased.

Simone gave her a tight smile. "Rise and shine."

"What time is it?" Emily asked.

"Late. After eleven."

"*Shit.*" Emily couldn't remember the last time she had slept that long. "Should I ask what day it is?"

Simone forced a laugh as she came over and sat on the edge of her bed.

"What is it?" Why do you look like that?"

"I finally figured it out," Simone said. "It was bugging the shit out of me all last night, but I woke up realizing why your father's picture looks so familiar."

"Why are we still on that?" Emily wasn't sure if she was elated or bothered. She should be happy, maybe even grateful Simone was interested in the connection. Emily might learn something new about her dad. But it was hard to feel eager about her mental investigation when she sensed something ugly in the tone of Simone's inquiry. "It's weird that you're obsessing over this."

"I'm not obsessing over anything. Your father looks familiar, naturally my brain wants to know why."

"And what did it come up with?" Emily asked, only half-wanting to know.

"Do you mind if I take another look before I say anything?"

Now Emily was really agitated. Just not enough to start an argument.

She rolled out of bed, stepped over the pair of pants lying in a puddle on the floor, trudged to the nightstand. The wallet was far closer to the lamp than where she had left it — definitely had been moved. She leafed through the cash, all of thirty-seven dollars and none of it touched. As she expected. Then she removed the old photo of her father from the zipper compartment.

It absolutely was not where she had left it.

Before she handed it to Simone, she made a show of holding it out of her reach. "Why do you want to see it?"

But Simone only held out her hand.

"Cut the shit. I know you looked at it last night."

"I did."

"Why?"

"I needed a closer look than the glance I got in the car."

"Why?"

"I told you why. It was familiar. I needed to see it. Think on it. Let it percolate while I slept."

"And?"

Simone extended her hand and tipped her head.

Reluctantly, Emily passed her the photo.

Simone took it, studied it. Glanced up at Emily then back down at the picture.

"Are you going to say anything?" Emily asked.

"I can't believe you don't see it. Or that it took me so long to. I was pretty sure last night, but now, in the light of day ..." She shrugged.

"See *what*?" Emily was getting agitated. Eleven or not, it was too early for some nonsense game of Guess Who? that she didn't want to play.

"Rick. Emily, he looks just like your father."

She snatched the picture away from Simone. Peered at it for several long seconds before meeting her handler's gaze. "There's a resemblance, sure. Maybe. Vague at best. If you squint. So what?"

"You've gotta be kidding. They look like brothers, Emily. *Close* brothers."

An involuntary laugh croaked out of her throat, barbed at the edges. "You're crazy."

Simone stared back at her, silent. Almost like she was afraid to talk.

"Why are you doing this? What's your point?"

Simone stayed calm, despite Emily's rising hysteria. "I don't have a point. It was just bothering me. In the car, when we were checking in. Even all last night. The dim lighting and short time frame still left me with doubts. But then I woke up, and it seemed so obvious. Rick doesn't just look like your father." She grabbed Emily's arms, turned her toward the sun, studied her face. "Emily — the two of you look like each other."

"Fuck you!" Emily bellowed, though she had no idea where the anger had come from, so sudden and thunderous.

"Calm down ." Simone raised her hands in surrender. "I'm not trying to fight with you, I just want to—"

"Wake me up and make me feel like shit for some reason." Now on her feet and full of energy, she started getting dressed.

"Please, Emily. This isn't necessary."

"But it's necessary to wake me up with the observation that my father looks like a criminal, and apparently so do I."

"I didn't wake—"

"You were pacing like a caged animal!"

"I was only trying to—"

"I know what you were trying to do, Simone!" Emily grabbed her phone then marched toward the door. She opened it, turned back, couldn't think of anything worth saying, then stormed into the hallway and let the door swing slowly and silently closed behind her.

A walk on the beach would probably help. The rational part of Emily's brain knew she was being unreasonable, but there was little she could do to quell her rising fury. Indignation. Outrage. Whatever it was she had felt from her former mentor's unnecessary insult.

She could see right through Simone's machinations. That bitch was up to her old tricks, trying to mess with her head, just like in Sniper School.

Emily just didn't know why.

She puzzled over Simone's motives while walking the

shoreline. Emily wasn't aimless, she was headed for the villa for some recon. It made sense to scope out their evening port of call while under a late morning sun. They were supposed to hook up with Rick, but right now Emily was glad to be alone and looking forward to maybe bringing back something the other two didn't have.

But she was too late for that. Once Emily was holding her shoes, toes buried in warm sand fronting the villa, she saw a small handful of professional executioners. She could see right through them. The man with his surfboard, the guy flying a kite, and Jackie-O might as well have been carrying signs. If there were three in sight, there were at least that many assassins still in the shadows.

Rick apparently preferred his recon solo, regardless of his promises. His back was to Emily, but it was definitely him. She finished pretending to take in the day then kept on walking.

Less than a minute later, a voice came from behind her. "Wait up!"

Rick, of course.

She turned around and found him smiling. Except this time, she couldn't stand to look at him. Didn't want to find out if it would feel like staring into a mirror. And she heard Simone like a specter in her head.

They look like brothers, Emily. Close brothers.

Rick doesn't just look like your father. Emily — the two of you look like each other.

"Where are you going?" Rick asked.

"I needed a walk."

"Or you were scoping Asher's villa and didn't want get spotted. You see me there?"

"Yes." No point in lying, especially as he wouldn't know if she was being truthful or not. "I didn't want to draw attention to either of us by saying hello. Why were you there? Weren't we supposed to meet up this morning?"

"We were, and I waited, but you didn't answer my texts, and I wasn't about to spend the day tickling myself."

"Oh. Sorry." Emily didn't need to look at her phone. She had grabbed it without even glancing at the screen before storming out of the room.

"*Sorry's* just a word, sunshine."

What was he trying to say? Emily finally forced herself to look at him. Right in his eyes. She tried to study him objectively, but even digging deep, she saw no resemblance. Maybe his love of crime was carved too deeply onto his features. Maybe objectivity was impossible if she saw only honor in her father and only disgrace in this mercenary.

"We just gonna stand here like assholes?" Rick asked.

"Did you find anything?"

"I always find something."

"When you were scoping out the villa. Specifically, then," Emily clarified.

"Why don't we head back to our hotel, and I'll tell you all about the nothing I saw?" Rick started walking.

Emily followed. "I thought you always found something."

"I found a redhead in a barely-there bikini who smelled ready to fuck."

"You're disgusting."

"It's a love-it-or-hate-it quality," Rick said.

"Does anybody love it?"

"I choose to spend time with people who appreciate the unique benefits of being around me."

"Have both of them ever been in the same room at once?" Emily asked.

Rick chuckled. "That's some serious life advice right there."

"What? Be an asshole and make sure you have a lot of money so everyone has to put up with your shit?"

"That. And that we are who we spend time with. It's better to be alone than in bad company."

Emily's heart stopped for a beat when he said that.

When it started again, everything changed.

Chapter Thirteen

"You're gonna have to repeat that," Rick said.

Emily had no idea what he was talking about. She couldn't remember the last several things out of her mouth. They were automatic responses, replies to whatever he was saying as her mind replayed his prior statement.

We are who we spend time with. It's better to be alone than in bad company.

Her father's words. Chilling enough without a morning spent arguing their physical resemblance.

It had to be a coincidence. Problem was, Emily didn't know if it was too big or small for that. She had no perspective. Was this some fate or providence intervening in her life? Or a random occurrence that meant nothing, Rick saying a phrase her father used to say. Maybe it came from the same root source. Or it was possible they were somehow related. Still, the relationship had to be distant. Rick couldn't be her brother unless Emily's dad had an affair before he died. That would make it more than an awfully unbelievable coincidence. It would also mean her life had been a lie. She wondered how old he was.

"Sorry," Emily finally responded. "I lost my train of thought."

"You ever consider that you might be shit at this job? No safe houses, flying coach, easily derailed thoughts. How long did you say you've been at this?"

There was something taunting in his tone, but Emily ignored it.

"Are you ready for tonight?" Rick asked, their hotel now about a hundred strides away.

"I will be." Emily wanted to say *yes*, but she knew Rick was looking for the truth.

"Anything I can do to help you?"

"Since when were you in the business of helping anyone?"

"I help those who happen to be helping me while also helping themselves. Right now, it seems that includes you, but it'll stop including you the second you become a liability. That's when I walk away. Continue to be a hindrance and I'll shoot your tits full of bullets."

He said it all so pleasantly. Like, *Yes, thank you. I would like a salad with that.*

"Thanks for the straight talk," Emily said.

"I knew you'd appreciate it. I hate the idea of hurting you, and I won't do it unless I have to. But it's fair for you to know it won't take much, seeing as my survival is an eternal concern. You should also know your appearance is atrocious this morning. You look like a Halloween costume."

They stepped from the sand to the hotel grounds.

"Where's your girlfriend?"

"She's not my girlfriend. Up in our room."

Rick gave her a lascivious grin. "Right. So, a drink?"

"It's barely even noon."

"Who gives a dick about that? You a slave to your

circadian rhythm or something?" Rick started walking inside, toward the bar. He turned back to Emily just slightly behind him. "You know the best time to drink?"

"When?" Emily asked, knowing the answer.

Whenever you want to.

"Whenever you want to." Rick laughed and kept walking.

Yes. There was something very familiar about him. But Emily had also spent a lot of time with the guy in the last day. He had a strong personality. The kind that steeped fast. This all made sense. Simone had gotten in her head this morning with that bullshit about their resemblance. She wouldn't be thinking about any of this otherwise.

"So, you joining me?" Rick asked, stopping at the bar.

Emily didn't want to spend another second with this man.

But she also wanted to know everything she possibly could about who he might be. The conversation could start out simply enough.

I know this sounds cheesy, but do we know each other from somewhere more than our meeting at the airport? You seem so familiar.

"One drink," Emily said.

"Before your girlfriend gets mad, sunshine?" He winked and took a seat.

"She's not my girlfriend. And stop calling me that." Emily sat beside him. "So, what do you drink before lunchtime? And don't say, *Whatever I want to.*"

"Well, that is the answer, but 'depends on the morning' is also correct."

"And this morning?"

"Watch," he said.

"How can I help you?" the bartender asked.

Rick leaned forward like he was about to spill a secret, but then he asked for one instead. "When's the last time you saw someone lose their shit? I don't mean tipsy, I mean you motherfuckers never should have served his ass and now he's out on the floor getting grabby and mouthy. I ain't no mystery shopper so you can—"

"I'm sorry, sir—"

Rick dropped a hundred on the table. "Sometimes I'm not clear. No trouble here, I'm not a lawyer or a cop or nothing. Just a fellow interested in a good story. I don't even need a name." He slid the bill forward. "So, when's the last time someone over-ordered and got a little too grabby?"

"About two weeks ago." The bartender swept his eyes across the landscape of humans, then quickly pocketed the bill. "Dude in his late twenties. He was DOA, drunk on arrival, but we went ahead and served him anyway. Guys like that over-tip, so you don't stop serving them. He was paying double for his drinks so none of us were saying no. But we had to after he tried to pull down one of the guest's bikini bottoms."

"Bold," Rick said with an appreciative nod. "What was he drinking?"

The bartender shook his head in apology. "A piña colada."

"We'll have two of those." Rick slapped his hand on the bar. "Bill my room, 1212."

The bartender looked confused, but then he reset himself with a nod. "Yes, sir."

Rick turned to Emily. "That's how I decided what to drink before lunchtime today."

"You're ridiculous. You just paid a hundred bucks for the bartender to tell you what to order. You could have just asked him for a suggestion. He would have given you one a lot better than that. Now you'll be drinking a piña colada. Two of them, in fact."

"I like piña coladas. You're gonna have to at least taste yours, and I bet you'll be glad for the panty grabber when you do. Because this place makes the fuck out of their old people drinks."

"Even so ... a hundred dollars."

"The fuck I care about a hundred dollars? I'm more offended by the price of our libations. Twenty-two bucks for a piña colada? That's bullshit. I paid for entertainment."

"How do you know how much they are, and really, that was entertaining for you?"

"I had one about an hour ago, and hell yeah, it's the gift that'll keep on giving. You know how many times I'll smile to myself thinking about that fucker wondering why I was asking about the guy who drank too much and got handsy? He'll ask himself if he missed something, if the guy is suing, or if someone is suing the guy. If he said or did anything he wasn't supposed to. Maybe contributed to the defendant's delinquency in some way, or to the plaintiff's trauma if that were the case." Rick laughed. "You see where I'm going with this?"

"You are truly a next level asshole."

"Two piña coladas," said the bartender, setting their drinks on the counter in front of them.

"Try it," Rick prompted once the bartender was gone.

Emily took a sip, willing to play for answers.

I know this sounds cheesy, but do we know each other from somewhere more than our meeting at the airport? You seem so familiar.

Best damn piña colada she'd ever tasted.

"Told you," Rick said.

She took another sip to buy another smile.

He pointed at his drink. "You can have mine if you want it."

"That's okay, thanks." Emily stopped drinking and

pushed her glass away from her on the counter. "I know this sounds cheesy, but do we know each other from somewhere?" She waited a beat then added, "From more than our meeting at the airport? You seem *so* familiar."

"You know, I was thinking the same—"

"Emily!"

She turned around to see Simone marching toward them.

"Told you your girlfriend was gonna get mad," Rick muttered with a satisfied chuckle.

Simone stopped in front of them, glaring at Emily. "You're drinking?"

"Not really," Emily said.

"Not unless piña coladas count," added Rick.

"We need to go. Come on." Simone stared at her, waiting.

"Where you ladies off to?"

Simone didn't answer.

"Yeah," Emily said. "Where are we going? We're supposed to be strategizing. Why don't you join us? The piña coladas here are amazing."

"We need to go shopping."

"Shopping for what?" Rick asked.

"None of your business. Come on, Emily."

"You better go, sunshine. It looks like she's about to spank you."

"I keep telling you how much I hate that," Emily said, imagining dragging a knife across his throat.

"And that's why I keep doing it."

He laughed, and Emily then imagined him healed so she could stain her thoughts picturing his open throat again.

Simone tugged at Emily. Now it was easy, as she wanted off the stool.

"You ladies wanna take these drinks with you?" Rick called out behind them, getting louder when they didn't answer. "See you later for the *you know what*."

Emily could hear him starting to laugh.

"That man is a pig," Simone said.

"No argument from me. But I was still getting somewhere, and you just marched right in and ruined it."

"And where were you getting, Emily? Explain it to me."

"I *just* asked him why he looked familiar."

Simone met her with a stony silence.

"What did I do now?" Emily asked, not needing an explanation.

"You still have so much to learn. I keep giving you the benefit of the doubt, telling myself and others you're ready when clearly you're not."

"You're only four years older than me, Simone."

"So, in other words, more than twice your experience."

Simone stopped in front of the elevator.

"I thought we were going shopping," Emily said.

"Have you seen yourself this morning?"

No more words were spoken until they were in their room, and then only barely. Emily went straight to the bathroom, and no shit, Simone and Rick were both right. She looked like a goblin. Like she killed children when they tried crossing her bridge.

She showered, felt ten times better, then got dressed and ready fast enough to impress Simone. Not that her handler acknowledged it. They barely talked while Simone drove her newest stolen car.

"Now you're just rubbing it in my face," Emily said. "We could have taken a FASTr."

"We need our own vehicle."

"If so, I'm sure there are other ways to make that happen."

"I'm sure, too. And not all of them fit with the plan."

"I can imagine how hard you tried." Emily dropped it. Didn't say another word until they turned onto Worth.

"You said we were going shopping. Why are we at the Rodeo Drive of Palm Beach?"

"You just answered your own question," Simone said.

Parking cost more than a pricy lunch for two. Emily was out of her element. Simone should have been, as well. But somehow, she knew exactly which stores to hit and precisely what to buy when they got there. The prices weren't just ridiculous, they were comical. Foolhardy, even. Who would spend that much for a dress? Especially one so ... revealing.

"You're paying cash?" Emily balked when Simone pulled out a wad of bills at the first place.

Simone turned to her, glaring.

She paid for their dresses, then scolded Emily outside. "You're going to blow our cover."

"How am I supposed to know we're undercover?"

"Assume we're always undercover. You're not acting the part."

"And how does one act the part, Simone?"

"Like someone who belongs wherever they are." She shook her head. "You really are an amateur."

That felt like an arrow sticking out of her side. Emily ignored it and said, "What's next?"

"We finish shopping. Shoes and makeup. I've secured us invitations to the party tonight, but we need to dress the part."

"The part of what? Hookers? I think you picked out the sluttiest dresses in the store."

"They're beautiful."

"Sure ... but—"

"Let's get on with it, Emily."

In the next shop, she asked Simone where the invitations had come from.

"We'll talk about it later," she said.

But back in the stolen car, Simone still didn't want to discuss it. Because she needed to focus on driving. Because it was a bigger conversation. Because the time wasn't right.

Because, *Jesus Christ will you just lay off and trust me?*

Hard to do when her handler was keeping secrets.

Back in the room, seeing all their clothes and accessories laid out, Emily felt unsettled. She grew less worried about the invitations or Simone's motivations and more about what might be expected of her at the evening festivities. The clothes cost a fortune and invited the kind of attention Emily had no intention of attracting.

"How did we get invited to this party, Simone?" Emily finally demanded, her tone unyielding.

"We're not *invited* so much as *working* it."

"What does that mean?"

"A party of escorts has been hired for the evening," Simone said. "And we're glomming onto that party."

Chapter Fourteen

SIMONE STARTED THE CAR.

"This is the third time he's texted," Emily said.

"I don't care if he texts another two-hundred times. Don't text him back."

"But he's on our side. For now."

Simone snorted.

"At least it's extra backup," Emily argued. "That's more than we have now."

"We're stronger if we know one of us isn't eventually going to betray the other two."

Emily struggled not to snort at the absurdity of that statement, given who uttered it. "We would do the same thing to him. You would for sure."

"The party is like two blocks away," Simone said. "I need you to put your party face on."

"I did that. It took over an hour. Remember? You made me watch all those videos before we even started? I said *this is stupid* about a hundred times?"

"Don't be a smart ass."

Emily said, "You act like I'm being unreasonable for

wanting more insight or insulation or protection. You're awfully cavalier about all of this. Maybe there's something you're not telling me?"

Simone was looking out at the road, but Emily would bet two toes that she rolled her eyes.

"No, there's nothing I'm not telling you, Emily. I don't trust Rick, and I wish you'd kept our conversation to yourself. You have a problem with boundaries."

Emily didn't respond. A few minutes later Simone pulled up to the valet, then they each got out of the car.

A gentleman in a tuxedo took their names. Simone had one for each of them, but both were new to Emily. Once given, he requested they please follow him. He led them down a regal hall with posh carpet and sky-high ceilings then through gardens that must have been bursting with butterflies in the daylight but in dusk were a medley of lush greenery amid the music of plinking water.

Finally, he took them outside to a boisterous riot of guests. "Please wait here. Ms. Malone will be right with you.

Then with a bow he was gone.

They stood at the top of the steps, surveying the crowded courtyard below. She had no idea who Ms. Malone was. Simone must, but Emily wasn't going to ask.

Simone turned from the courtyard to Emily. "Recognize anyone?"

"Not yet. It's impossible to know who's here to kill and who's here to die."

"We came here to kill. Maybe—"

"*There.*" Emily murdered her thought with an urgent whisper. She didn't want to point, so she nodded toward the man standing by the bar with a smirk that seemed as part of his face as the blond belonged to his longish hair. "He's in a tux, Simone."

"So what? A lot of the male guests are wearing tuxes. This is that kind of party."

"Exactly. The *guests* are wearing tuxes. And no matter what Rick is wearing, there he is." Again, Emily nodded toward the stranger who had suddenly become an unshakable part of her life. "He's been trying to reach us all day. We could have been his plus-ones instead of coming to this soiree as hookers."

"Maybe *you* could have. I doubt he'd have more than one guest, and we both know who he'd have chosen. More to the point, you need to stop calling us hookers. We're escorts. You don't have to let anyone do anything to you. It's just our cover."

"It's like you've given me a warm blanket to smother all my doubts," Emily said. "Thank you, Mommy."

"Allison? Amelia?"

They turned to see a small woman with big eyes looking at them expectantly.

"I'm Ms. Malone," she said with a smile. "Please, follow me."

She started down the stairs, and they followed several steps behind.

"Who is she?" Emily finally asked.

"A facilitator."

"You mean a madame."

"If you insist on using that terminology, then yes," Simone said.

"So, this is an illegal high-end prostitution ring. We let it go on so we can dip into the information channels when and wherever we need to."

"Close enough."

"Please, wait here until someone has use for you." Ms. Malone gave them another formal nod that in no way matched her belittling words.

"What do you mean 'until someone has use for us'?" Emily asked.

"When one of the party's guests decides that time with you is more valuable than time spent elsewhere and decides to do something about it," she clarified.

Then Ms. Malone grazed her with another once-over that suggested Emily had nothing to worry about and left.

"I'm glad we're escorts instead of hookers," Emily said once Ms. Malone was out of earshot.

Simone didn't respond.

But Ms. Malone was right. Emily probably didn't have anything to worry about. Every woman in the alcove looked like a model, except for Simone, and she was much closer than Emily. Blondish brown hair, intelligent eyes, and a spray of freckles across her nose. But better than anything, Simone's swagger wafted right off of her. She acted like she had lived through her twenties twice already.

"What happens if we leave the alcove?" Emily asked.

"I assume we're being watched. Our best bet is to get out of this area and into the general population."

"You mean the general population of one-percenters. By way of someone paying to fuck us."

"You don't have to do anything you don't want to do."

"So you keep saying. I have zero chance of getting picked, so we need a Plan B."

"Someone here is looking for exactly what you have to offer."

"I don't have anything to offer anyone," Emily said. "Not like that."

"Bullshit," Simone said, then promised to show Emily what she meant.

But she never got a chance. Or maybe Simone used her first chance a little too well and made it her only one. Because a gentleman entered the alcove and surveyed the selection with hungry eyes. He passed over everyone twice, but the second time he settled on Simone for some reason Emily couldn't, or at least didn't, understand.

Simone took a bold step forward, and the gentleman did the same. His hand went out, hers went in it, then together they left the alcove. Simone didn't even turn to acknowledge Emily on the way out.

She weighed her options. There was zero chance she was waiting around in the alcove all night. She needed to split. Even if someone was watching, Emily felt confident that she could disappear into the crowd. Maybe find a man to shield her if needed, but on her terms. Not someone taking a stroll back to where the whores were stored to select one for some scheduled depravity. That wouldn't be good for anyone. She'd end up cutting the guy's dick off and maybe gutting his body. His dying screams would draw too much attention.

Another man entered the alcove. Longish blond hair and a smirk.

But this guy wasn't a gentleman, and he didn't survey the crowd. He walked right up to Emily. "I saw your girlfriend leaving with some guy, so I figured …"

"Do I get to leave with you?" Emily whispered.

"I think that's how it works."

Rick made a hoop with his arm for Emily to loop hers through. He ushered her out of the alcove, across the courtyard, then upstairs into a bedroom.

He closed the door behind them.

"Thank you for saving me, but—"

"Shut up." Rick grabbed Emily by the arm then threw her onto the bed.

She held her momentum, rolled to the other side. Landed on her feet, arms up and fists out in fighting position. "What the hell is wrong with you?"

"You first. We had a deal. So why did y'all try to cut me out of it?

"That was only one of us. I saw all of your texts and wanted to answer them. Simone wouldn't let me."

"*She wouldn't let you?* That ain't how life works, sunshine. We are each responsible for own actions."

"I'm here now. We can still make a plan."

"No deal." He shook his head. "I don't trust your judgment."

"What's wrong with my judgment?"

"Your girlfriend is what's wrong with your judgment. You have to stand for what's right, Emily. Even if it means standing alone." Rick drew a breath before delivering a finishing line that felt like a finishing move. "The honorable are always accountable to their own code of conduct."

There was something going on here that Emily didn't understand, and there had been from the beginning.

"Why are you hitching your cart to my horse?"

Rick laughed. "My cart to your horse, huh? That what you call my safe house, my transportation, my connections, and my eternal patience?"

"No. It's what I call the something you know about my family."

His face was blank.

"Is your name really Rick?"

No answer.

"How do we know each other?" Emily asked. "So, what? You're just not going to answer me?"

"You need to stop the bullshit and remember we're here for the safe."

"Good luck. I don't know how to pick a safe. Simone was going to take care of that part."

"I can handle the safe, but you need to take care of Asher."

"You mean kill him."

"No," Rick said, "I mean take him to a fancy Mexican restaurant where they make tableside guacamole, and I need you to make sure and order the deep-fried ice cream."

"In case you haven't noticed, I'm dressed like a whore. Not a lot of room for a gun in this getup."

"You telling me you don't know how to kill a fucker without a gun?"

"Sure, but—"

"You need to get creative and figure it out fast. We want the Zip file and the target tonight. *We* means you and me, just so we're clear. I've been trying real hard to help you out and have been having a hell of a time with it. I'm not sure how much longer I'll be willing to carry with the burden. Let's just say, if you turn on me again, run back to your girlfriend, or do anything else to undermine our current agreement—"

"You'll kill me?"

He laughed. "I won't have to. I'll rat you out to our target instead. And Amil. Then they can go to war over who gets to finish you off."

"Rat me out for what?" Emily challenged him.

"Wanna take your pick?" Rick held her against his mocking smile.

It worked. Emily had no idea if he was bluffing. But really, right now, she didn't have much of a choice. "Fine. I'll take care of the target. But you need to get me a gun. I bet you have one on you now."

"No can do," Rick said. "You'll take care of the target or the target will take care of you. I'm not arming you either way."

"How do you expect me to do anything without a gun?"

He raked his gaze across Emily's body, head to toe and back. "Look him in the eyes then get down on your knees and keep on looking up at him. I'm sure you'll think of some way to exploit his vulnerability." He laughed and added, "I have faith in you, sunshine."

"That's the last time. Next time I really will kill you."

"Then I'll make sure it's a good one."

And Emily said, "I don't care if it is."

Chapter Fifteen

EMILY WAS sure Asher had a last name, but according to Rick, no one at the party seemed to know it.

Before Rick left, Emily had said to him, "Where am I supposed to find this guy? I don't even know what he looks like." It wasn't like Amil had shown them a photo.

His clever response had pissed her off.

"Figure the rest out for your goddamned self." He sighed when she glared at him. "Asher's been in the hot tub since the party started, so far as I know he hasn't gone anywhere. I'd start there."

Her dress was revealing, but still had a lot more coverage than even most of the bikinis at this party. Emily was wondering how she would get near the water in her gown, let alone compete with whatever women happened to be vying for Asher's attention.

Emily found the hot tub in a perfectly shaded grotto, along with the launderer and a much larger problem than she'd anticipated. Asher was the only male in the hot tub, and he was also the only one dressed. The five women sharing his bubbles had flesh that varied in color from flour to cinnamon, but all were centerfold naked. Two were draped over him, one on either side, with another on his lap and a pair off to the side making out, even though Emily would have gladly bet her favorite sniper rifle it was all a display, and neither were gay.

Asher could give a shit about the random partygoer who had wandered over to his much smaller and more intimate celebration in the back. He didn't so much as look up or glance over. Emily had no idea how she would get his attention.

She looked behind her, saw a passing waiter, scurried over to his tray, and grabbed two glasses of champagne. She downed the first, then started spilling the second flute of liquid courage down her throat.

Back in the grotto, Emily set one of her glasses on the ground and approached the hot tub in a ridiculous sashay, still holding the second glass and hoping that Asher would look up so she could quit her facade.

She got right up to the water and kicked off a shoe, then she dipped her toe into the hot tub and flicked a stream of water toward the writhing bodies.

Asher finally looked up. "Can I help you with something?"

Emily held up her empty glass and intentionally, but lightly, slurred her words. "I want another drink. And since it looks like you're the man of the hour, I was hoping I could have it with you."

Asher pushed the redhead off of his lap. She took the hint and drifted away with the blonde and brunette by her side, all of them now floating over to join the couple making out.

"Why don't you take that off and get in here. I'll have a bottle brought over."

Emily held Asher's stare. "That's not what I was thinking."

"It wasn't, huh? And what were you thinking? Because looking at you now, maybe you seem a bit too high strung for what I have in mind."

Asher was slurring his words too, but not on purpose. He wasn't wasted out of his mind, but the guy was fuckered enough to believe Emily was interested instead of suspicious.

She sauntered around to his side of the hot tub, using her dress and the body inside it as a prop, and managed to show Asher more than the bimbos in the water while also showing him less.

"I'm not uptight at all." Then closer to him, and in more of a whisper, said, "I promise, I'm in the mood for *exactly* what you have in mind."

That did it. Asher lit right up. Emily didn't know what the asshole was thinking about, but it was clearly on his mind now. She could see the evidence tenting his swim trunks. She had somehow managed to do what the bimbos in the water had not. Asher was probably just curious. Her being more of a mystery enhanced his desire.

He told the bimbos to scram as he lumbered out of the water. Took him no time at all to don a robe, then he dragged his lurid gaze across her body again. "You sure we can't" — he looked around the grotto — "you know?"

As breathy as she could, she replied, *"In your room, please."*

Asher slipped his feet into his shoes with a shrug, then he led her out of the grotto, up the steps, then back through the crowd. As she wove through the throng, she looked for Rick or Simone or anyone else she might recognize — even Salsa might have felt like a port in the storm. But Emily saw no one as she left the party behind her. Her stomach roiled as she ascended the stairs toward a waiting bedroom three steps behind the man she was there to eliminate.

The movie played in her mind, imagining what she would do the second Asher laid a hand on her. She had been waiting for this. Her blood was warm, and her body was hot. Just not in the way her mark wanted it to be.

Only the two of them rode the elevator. Emily could imagine what he was thinking and longed to inch away from him. But she swayed almost drunkenly toward his body instead.

As they made their way down the hallway, she let him walk a step ahead. Asher stopped at his door and looked back at her — lecherous and lewd, his indecency barely disguised. He would pop the top once he got Emily into his room.

Asher opened the door, held it open for her. Once Emily entered, he slipped inside then closed the door behind her.

He beckoned her as he walked backward toward the overstuffed sofa. It might have been the nicest piece of furniture she had ever seen. The place looked more like a palace wing than anything rented by the night. An identical robe to the one he had on was draped over the arm. Asher had used this sofa for exactly this same thing before, and recently.

This asshole probably spent a third of each day ejaculating.

"You coming?"

"I will be." Emily offered him a whore's smile, even though the mask felt like it might crack her actual face.

"How am I gonna get undressed if you don't undress me?" Asher had already untied his belt. Now, he looked down at his swim trunks and thrust his pelvis toward her.

She swallowed her revulsion. "Undress your goddamned self."

That one felt good to say, and Asher seemed to like it.

His robe hit the floor, then his trunks. He was fully erect and smiling expectantly. "Your turn."

It sure was, but Emily might not be ready for this. He was fully aroused, his cock throbbing. His eyes gleamed as he hunched forward, sweat and water still beading much of his body.

She had been in dangerous situations before, but nothing like this. In a few seconds, he would learn what Emily was there to do. Asher laundered money for some of the most dangerous men in the world. If she made even the smallest mistake, dying wouldn't be the worst of it. That atrocity belonged to all the awful ways her would surely defile her body, first while her heart was still beating, then maybe again even after it wasn't.

They were six feet apart.

Emily had exactly one chance.

"This dress is so thin—" she ran a finger along the side of it "—I wonder if you could rip it right off of me."

Asher grinned, getting what she wanted him to do even if he misunderstood the why.

He came toward Emily, his erection like an angry arrow aimed at her heart, hungry hands out as if they were going to maul her.

But Emily grabbed him by the wrist, yanked it as hard as she could behind his back, circling around and slamming her foot into the crook of the launderer's knee.

Asher vented an inhuman bellow.

She pushed up harder on his arm, an inch from it cracking, then used his pain and her weight to land them both on the floor.

"That's the only one you get," she breathed hard into

his ear. "Yell like that again and I'll kill you. Grunt if you understand me."

Asher grunted.

"Now grunt like a pig because I told you to."

He refused, so Emily pushed up on his arm, eating half of the inch that kept it from breaking and making the pain that much more excruciating.

Asher grunted like a pig.

Emily relaxed her hold. "I'm going to need the combination to the safe, or I'll kill you."

"Whatever you say." For the first time, Asher sure as hell sounded sincere.

"Does this room have any weapons?" Emily narrowed her eyes at him. "I'll kill you for lying same as anything else."

"There's a knife in the nightstand. Can I get dressed?"

"Good idea," Emily said, already on her way to the nightstand.

Asher went for the nearest robe on the arm of the sofa instead of his trunks, turning his back to Emily as he dressed, thankfully hiding his hardon. The fear of God had apparently swollen it even more. Or maybe it had been her body pressed against him.

His arms were through the sleeves, but they sure as hell weren't tying the belt.

"What are you doing?" Emily yelled.

"Nothing," Asher grunted.

"Stop that! Right fucking now!"

"Almost done …"

Then, with his back to her, he suddenly was.

"I should kill you for that," she said.

"It's over now."

She curled her lip, disgusted. "Take me to the safe."

He led Emily into his study, where he seemed just as

surprised as she was to see Rick and Simone kneeling over the safe. Emily didn't bother with *what are you guys doing here?* or any other cliché. Instead, she nodded at each of them and said, "I brought someone to help you with that."

Asher looked back at her, and she nudged him forward with the knife.

He ignored Emily, walked over to the safe, kneeled when he got there, then turned swiftly around as he drew a gun from his robe.

He barely aimed and fired.

Simone screamed.

Rick drew his gun.

Emily leapt at Asher. On him in a second, she tackled the asshole then held her knife to his balls.

Rick took three strides up to Asher then shoved the barrel of his gun into the man's temple.

"Don't!" Emily cried out.

"Gimme one reason."

"He can still open the safe." She looked over at Simone, clutching her thigh in what was surely a painful but clearly non-lethal wound.

"You have two seconds, Hefner."

Emily let the launderer go then watched him crawl over to the safe. Once open, Rick slammed the back of Asher's head with the butt of his gun. "You get to live another few minutes while I see if I have any questions about whatever I find in here. Why don't you worm your way over to the corner and enjoy it."

Emily left them to check on Simone in the adjoining bathroom, already cleaning her wound.

"Are you okay?"

Simone looked up. "I'll be fine." Then without waiting for Emily's response, "Get back out there. You need to control the situation."

"But—"

"Now."

Emily returned to the study. Simone was right. Rick was already done and standing over a whimpering Asher. A few more seconds and she would have been too late for good.

"Stop it!" she called out.

Rick looked over, his attention still half on Asher, the gun still frighteningly close to his face.

"You didn't get to spend as much time with this asshole as I did. The fucker just jerked off right in front of me. I want to finish him."

"That was a distraction!" Asher defended himself. "I was only trying to get the gun."

"That should help your case," Rick said, looking artificially impressed.

"He's mine." Emily took out her knife.

"Have at him. But his balls'll probably bleed worse than you think."

"Lie down," she ordered.

Simone came out of the bathroom but didn't say a word.

Asher laid all the way down on the floor.

"Play Jesus," Emily ordered. "Arms out."

He did as Emily instructed. Then she straddled him and mouthed the words, *play dead*.

His eyes widened and she mouthed it again.

"Right in the heart," Emily announced while bringing the blade down.

But that wasn't where it landed. She buried it slightly higher to avoid Asher's heart and lungs, then got off his body and said, "Let's get the hell out of here."

Then they did.

Chapter Sixteen

EMILY REALLY WISHED Rick would stop complimenting her murder.

But ever since they left Asher's place, the asshole wouldn't shut up about it.

"Too bad there wasn't a mirror so you could see yourself," Rick kept going on and on, that last time making her want to sock him in the ear. "You were practically drooling. Remind me not to ever try and fuck you."

Then he laughed yet again like the asshole he was.

Simone stayed mostly silent. Emily's chest felt even heavier than the rest of her body.

They were finally on their way to the Breakers, their original supposed destination before getting rerouted to the Japanese Gardens. They left their car with the valet, found the Uniform Ensemble Company on the directory, then followed the manicured path to a cluster of small tables and empty chairs. A horde of restless killers milled about, all on their feet. One empty podium stood in the front of the room.

"Cool it, soldier," Simone whispered to Emily.

"I'm not doing anything."

"You're drenched in sweat."

"I'm not *drenched.*"

"You need to look like you have your shit together more than you do."

"I feel like something awful is about to happen," Emily said.

"No one is even armed."

"How do you know?"

"We were frisked," Simone said. "Remember?"

"Sure, we were. How do we know about all of them?"

"You're probably right. There's going to be a bloodbath. So be ready."

Emily looked at Simone. "I can't tell if you're mocking me."

Simone shrugged. "I'm not sure, either."

The next hour was excruciating, and even with that first one behind them, the podium was still empty.

No Amil the next hour, either. Heading into the third, Emily fretted a massacre. Most of the assassins were here *just in case.* Emily wondered if some of the guests staring out at the ocean right now were planning to kill the winner just because it wasn't them.

Salsa looked calm. But a few feet away from him stood a man with a very square head, rounded out by a sloping beard beneath his chin. His eyes were murderous, and his mouth was twisted into a homicidal smile. Jackie-O stood there, boiling between them.

Emily wondered about each of these killer's stories. Everyone here had to have gone through something. Why hadn't any of them managed to kill Asher? They were professional assassins, and it wasn't like Emily even had the comfort of her rifle. She had managed to maneuver the launderer into his bedroom though no one else had. Again, everything struck Emily as a little too convenient.

Another agonizing half-hour moved the emotional temperature to sweltering, despite the overly polite waiting staff and constantly refilled beverages.

Finally, Amil took the stage, still shirtless and still without a hair on his body.

But this time, their host looked upset. Again, he paced the stage, but differently than he had before. It sounded almost like spitting when he finally spoke.

"The Foreman has been disheartened by all of you." Amil stopped pacing then stood there shaking his head. "Is there anyone here with anything worthy to claim?"

It was only a flicker within a moment, but Emily could swear she saw something pass between Rick and Amil. A shit eating aura from Rick, and an accusatory glance from Amil.

"Here here." Rick raised a lazy right hand, the shit eating air making its way into his smile. "Your man is currently going through a severe case of rigor mortis, and the Zip drive's in a secure location."

Amil stared out at the crowd. "So, I'm to understand that *Meteor here*" — he said it like something was rotting on his tongue — "is the only one who got close to the target?"

Restless murmurs through the crowd, but no one spoke. The way they were all staring at Rick, Emily wanted none of the credit and wished she and Simone weren't standing so close to him.

"Can *anyone* here claim *any* points?" Amil's muscles were visibly tight. He was upset, and Emily didn't understand why. Something was happening that didn't make sense, and it felt somehow hidden in plain sight.

When the courtyard stayed silent, Amil gestured to the open bar. "You are all dismissed. Enjoy a final drink on your way out." Then he turned to Rick. "You, over here."

Rick gave Emily and Simone a smile that still seemed out of place. Then he cast it onto a crowd that clearly wanted to kill him, ignoring their collective ire as he swaggered toward the stage.

"We're going to get murdered just for standing next to him," Emily whispered to Simone.

"We'll be fine."

Five minutes of silence passed while the women worked to stay invisible. A few of the assassins left or found their place in the shadows. Several milled about. Emily wondered if they were in any real danger. Surely there had to be some code of honor among mercenaries. Rick wasn't going to die just because he won, and they weren't about to get killed for knowing him. That was just Emily's mind playing tricks. An overactive imagination swearing that Cosmo and Salsa were whispering on the lawn, trying not to look Emily's way while plotting to kill her.

"What do you think they're talking about?" Emily finally asked, nodding toward Rick and Amil.

Simone turned to her. "Oh, now we're allowed to communicate?"

"I wasn't shushing you, I just didn't want the attention. Now, what do you think they're talking about?"

"I don't know, but it looks like a vein is about to pop on Amil's forehead."

"Rick doesn't look bothered."

"Does he ever?"

"But aren't you curious what it is that could make Amil so mad? Why doesn't he just kick Rick out of the contest if he's pissed at him about something?"

"Because he doesn't have the power," Simone said. "Obviously."

"It doesn't make sense. Amil is acting on the Foreman's behalf, right? So why would he want to put up with Rick's brand of bullshit?"

"Why don't you get closer and try to find out?" Simone suggested.

"You do it."

"I would, but you're the one with the relationship. It'll look like you're waiting on him if you get closer. But I'll look like I'm trying to eavesdrop."

She might as well have added, *And that's an order.*

So, Emily inched closer.

And closer. Another series of steps. Then a few more.

Finally, she was within hearing distance.

"—keep tabs on things for your father, not enter the contest for yourself. This is—"

Amil stopped talking. A tentative, haphazard smile found his agitated face. Turning to Emily he said, "I'm sorry, may I help you?"

"No, I'm sorry. It's nothing." She smiled, offered a small bow of her head, then slowly backed away, leaving the men to their argument.

"What is it?" Simone asked once Emily was back beside her. Then, in a whisper, "*Are you shaking?*"

"I'm fine."

"What is it?"

"Not now," Emily said.

"Now is exactly when you need to spill it, and that's an order. What did you just hear?"

"Rick …" Emily swallowed. "He's been playing us the entire time."

"What do you mean — how has he been playing us?"

"I don't know." She shook her head. "But he's supposed to have been keeping tabs on 'things,' and I think those things are us."

"Tabs for who?"

"For his father." Emily glanced over at Rick and Amil. Their postures had relaxed, and it looked like the argument was settling.

"The guy who owns the chain of Pier One knockoffs?"

"I'm not saying it makes any sense."

"Why would Rick help us?" Simone asked. "If he was supposed to be helping us, then why would he—"

"I have no idea, but that's what Amil was saying to him. That he wasn't supposed to enter the contest for himself."

"What else did he say?"

"That's it. That he was supposed to be keeping tabs on us for his father and not entering the contest. That's when Amil saw me and stopped talking."

Looking lost in thought, Simone didn't respond.

"Any ideas who Rick's father might be?" Emily asked.

"No, not yet." But her voice was strained. Her body, rigid.

Simone was lying.

Emily was about to dig deeper when Amil raised his hand then waited for one of them to notice. Simone noticed him first, then redirected Emily's attention. Once they were both looking, Amil waved them over.

Rick stood between them as Amil delivered their final objective.

For this last job, they would need to be on their own. There would be no team-ups, and only one person would earn the prize at the end — a permanent and high-ranking position in the Outfit.

"So, what's the job?" Rick asked, with a sneering tone that further convinced Emily the asshole already knew.

"There is a traitor among us," Amil said. "Whomever finds and kills that betrayer will earn the position."

Chapter Seventeen

"Consider him dead," Simone said, staring at Rick.

He grinned back at her.

Rick knew something, but she wasn't sure what. He was surveying the situation, looking from Simone to Emily and back, his eyes alight with indecision. He smiled wider, the truth of what he knew, or didn't, desperate to bleed out.

This might very well be the end of her life. Both of their lives. And the Outfit wouldn't make it easy. She and Simone would be tortured. Pure brutality, and all for nothing in the end.

Emily had only seconds.

Rick nodded at Simone. He swiveled his head to offer Amil an expression that said, *Wanna know a secret?* Then he opened his mouth and—

Emily was on him, yanking Rick back into a chokehold as a startled Amil fell a full step back. Her fist pounded into Rick's chest. Ripped all the air from his body and made him collapse against her. She held him up and raised her knife to his throat.

A Simple Kill

"Whoa ..." His feet scrabbled on the lawn, body tensing as if only then realizing the severity of this situation. "Hold up, sunshine. We—"

Emily dragged the blade across his throat, opening Rick's skin like a zipper.

Blood poured out like liquid from the bottom of a busted bucket, but still Emily held his body against her as a shield, yelling, "I got your traitor!"

But Amil was aghast, pulling a phone from a pocket in pants that looked like they had none.

Two swipes then the phone was to his ear, the moderator of this nightmare now calling for backup.

Emily turned to Simone. "Run."

"We need to—"

"*RUN!*"

Simone turned and hightailed without argument after that.

The nick of time. Emily was surrounded less than a minute later. The assassins had split. Not one of them had entered the fray, scattering like cowards instead.

She hoped Simone was safe. Kept telling herself her handler had gotten free as the armed men and women closed in around her. She supposed there were both men and women. The bodies seemed to suggest it, though the all-black getups and matching black masks made it hard to know for sure. All that military gear at The Breakers, on a lawn that had hosted an endless parade of lavish weddings through the eras. It was all as out of place as the assault rifles aimed at Emily, the corpse she had left on the lawn at her feet, or its blood she could smell, like burning aluminum pluming into her nostrils.

She dropped her knife and raised her hands high. Then Emily got down on her knees. Slowly, she flattened herself onto the ground, palms pressed to the back of her head.

After her wrists were bound and she was raised to her feet, Emily made her Hail Mary, looking at Amil as she announced, "I got him! I got the traitor!"

But she hadn't, and everyone knew it.

And now she was on her way to die.

"You have made a terrible mistake," Amil said as they led Emily away.

"No shit." She didn't know how else to respond.

He shook his head. "You have no idea."

Emily was put into a car, with Amil in the seat beside her. She asked him several questions, but he didn't answer even one during their hour and a half drive to Miami. Not until they were pulling up to a stunning piece of modern architecture that had only become visible once they passed the tall stone gate, which in itself looked like a museum piece.

"Where are we?" Emily asked as their driver passed the gate.

"This is the Foreman's Miami home. He has requested your presence."

Back to back, those were the two most violently frightening sentences Emily had ever heard. She went to open the car door, but Amil grabbed her by the arm, his grip gentle but insistent.

"What is it?" Emily asked.

His eyes were—

Was he afraid for her?

"There is no way to prepare you for ..." Amil stopped, he swallowed and shook his head, suddenly refusing to finish his thought. Then he took a breath and seemed to reset himself. "There is no way to prepare you for what you are about to experience."

"You mean meeting the Foreman? I'm sure he's not that special."

Amil stared back at Emily, his eyes icy with all the things he could not or would not say. Then he let her go.

She opened the door. Almost spilled onto the ground. Begrudgingly, she waited for him.

He led her past another pair of guards at the entrance, up a wide set of stairs, down a hallway to the right at the top, then directly to a door at the very end.

"I won't be going in there with you," Amil announced when they arrived.

"You can't, or you won't be?"

"It isn't my place." Amil knocked on the door four times, each with a precise beat between it and the next one. Before the door was opened, he made an about face then began walking back down the hall.

There was a dull *thunking* sound, like tumblers relaxing inside a lock. The door sighed as if inviting Emily in. With a heart that felt like it might pound through the floor, she turned the knob then opened the door.

Hers was a terror of momentum instead of paralysis. That was the only reason Emily managed to spill into the room. Her heart stopped exactly one step inside. There was a pregnant, impossible second. She had to be seeing things, so she blinked into the surreality then stared.

She was standing before a man wearing a costume made to look like her father.

But despite how desperately she clung to that notion, she knew it to be false.

He was older, about ten years or so, with a trim beard her dad had never worn. But his eyes were the same, and his mouth, lips pursed at her like they always used to be. The man who might be her father was instantly on his feet then in front of his desk. He took a step toward her, his features becoming more and more clear as he approached.

It couldn't be, but it was.

Her knees buckled. Emily collapsed to the floor, smacking her head because she hadn't the wherewithal to even try and break her fall.

Through the pain, she stared up at both nightmare and dream while sprawled at his feet.

Then he was kneeling beside her. And he pulled Emily — his daughter? — into his arms.

"Are you okay?"

A tear slid down her cheek as she asked, "Are you my father?"

He answered by holding her against his chest and petting her hair. "I've missed you so much."

He planted his lips on the back of her head, and for one beautiful moment, all was right with the world.

But Emily was swimming, and the current was moving against her. She feared drowning in it.

She drew a deep breath to regain control, then she steadied herself to start over.

Painful as it was, she pulled away from her father's embrace. "Why are you here?"

"I've been watching over you for a long time now. Even pulled a few strings here and there."

But that wasn't an answer. Emily asked herself how this could be happening

Her father was the Foreman? The monster running the Outfit?

Instead of being dead, he ran the fastest growing criminal organization in America?

It was a wallop, accepting her DNA was as diseased as anyone's while grieving the father she never really had.

He led her to a chair, and she sat without argument.

Then he pulled his chair next to her and took a seat beside her, waiting for her to break the silence.

"How did this happen?" she finally asked.

Her father reclined in his seat with a shrug. "It's simpler than you probably think."

But Emily leaned forward, her jaw firming. "I'm sure I deserve to hear every word."

The whole conversation felt as surreal as the moment her mind had to accept what her eyes insisted. It hit her in a fog, fragments of her father's impossible story striking like lightning inside her.

"You have been ... misled," he started. "I was the prisoner of a cartel, not a foreign government. The Army acted like I was KIA, but they knew what really happened to me. They had to."

Emily could see the bitterness on his lips. That's what had started it all — that his country had known he'd been taken yet they'd never tried to rescue him, choosing to let him rot with his captors instead.

"But I'm a survivor, and so I survived," he told her. "The capo, DeSilva, respected me enough to keep me alive. And when he needed one of his enemies eliminated, I was happy to do that favor for him, seeing as those same enemies were some of the individuals responsible for my making DeSilva's acquaintance in the first place."

Her father told her all about how one favor led to another, until eventually he and DeSilva were spending the majority of their days talking shit. He became instrumental in DeSilva's organization, and eventually encouraged him to splinter off from the trunk of a multi-family framework and start a rebrand with the Outfit. DeSilva got capped, then there were several capos after that, each one acting as the Foreman for a tenure before getting eliminated. The cycle continued until a former Army sniper claimed the title for himself and brought an insider's intelligence to the organization.

"So, you used your government contacts to try and bring the government down?" Emily asked.

"We're not trying to bring the government down. We just need to make sure we can topple the support columns whenever we want to so they're never in our way."

"Plus, all the revenge." Emily hated that she sounded like a petulant teenager, but she hated what her father was doing even more.

"Of course." He looked at her without apology. "This contest was a way for me to find an entry point into the government, learn exactly who knew what was happening to me, then eliminate them."

"Was Rick really your son?"

A nod. "He was."

Voice cracking. "But I killed him."

A careless shrug. "It was worth the trade."

"You're okay with your son dying?" Emily couldn't believe her ears.

"It wasn't my first choice."

She shook her head. "You're nothing like him ... like the father I knew."

"You were a little girl. I'm exactly the same."

"No ..." still shaking her head. "You *feel* different. You never loved me."

"Of course I loved—"

"You let us think you were dead! It destroyed Mom!"

"I couldn't come home, Emily. And your mother was always frail. You can't blame her weakness on me."

She bolted up from her seat and stared at her father, wanting to flee his study but wondering if he would slaughter her for making the attempt.

"You're here now, and that isn't an accident. I've

brought you here. Rick was supposed to keep an eye on you. It—"

"Why?"

"Tepper was the last person on my list. With your brother dead, a position in the Outfit has opened up, even higher than the one you were auditioning for. This is a family business, Emily. We would make a great team."

"I don't want anything to do with you." Tears fell but she didn't wipe or acknowledge them.

"It takes time to adjust. I felt the same way about DeSilva. But things change, Emily. Life gets better." Her father pulled a phone from his pocket then swiped his thumb across the glass. Soon, his office door opened. Two men came entered the study, dragging a captive between them. They stopped by his desk then tossed their prisoner onto the floor.

Tepper growled but said nothing.

The Foreman stood, opened a desk drawer, produced a gun. He circled his desk, paused in front of the colonel, then with a lackadaisical crouch, pressed the gun to her head.

"I knew it was you," Tepper snarled.

"No." The Foreman shook his head. "I don't think you did."

Tepper spat. The Foreman wiped it off his face, pressed the barrel harder against her skull, and—

Emily tackled him and sent the gun flying as Tepper scrambled for cover.

The men who dragged her inside were still in the room.

"Stay back! Don't shoot!"

But the Foreman yelled a second too late. A pair of shots thundered through the room, explosions scattering shrapnel splinters as two bullets ripped into the mahogany desk.

Emily was wrestling with her father — or the Foreman, she had to keep reminding herself — as she worked to retain the power position. He seemed reluctant to hurt her, but she had no such qualms. She smashed her elbow down onto his nose and cracked the bridge.

He cried out as his eyes filled with blood.

Emily made a run for the gun.

Bullets flew everywhere, even though the boss had ordered his men to hold their fire.

Emily grabbed the pistol, rolled onto her back. She scooted toward the wall as she surveyed the situation.

The shooting had stopped for a reason. Her father's — *the Foreman's* — men were corpses on the floor. Simone stood in the doorway, gun in hand, blood blooming across her abdomen.

She collapsed with a whimper.

Emily heard the sound of a safety flicked off behind her.

She turned to see the Foreman raising a pistol and turning toward Tepper, still tied up on the floor.

But Emily raised hers, too.

She pulled the trigger then watched her father die.

Chapter Eighteen

"I'm sorry I didn't trust you," Emily said.

Simone didn't answer, even after Emily squeezed her hand.

"She'll be fine," the nurse worked to reassure her again. "She's just unconscious."

"I know." Now Emily felt embarrassed. She hadn't known Julia was in the room, so it felt like she had just been caught talking to herself. "Do you think she'll wake up soon?"

Julia didn't make Emily feel self-conscious. Instead, she patted her gently on the shoulder. "Soon enough." Then she left her alone with Simone.

It stayed quiet for the next hour. Emily kept squeezing Simone's hand, hoping she would wake up, wanting to hear her voice or get the chance to say she was sorry, to promise she would trust her mentor forever.

The door opened. Emily looked over, expecting to see Julia again.

But it was Tepper, her face somber and knowing. She

bowed in deference, this time with no chaperones by her side.

"I wanted to tell you," the colonel said, her eyes full of apology. "But they wouldn't let me."

"I understand."

"For the record, Simone didn't know," Tepper added.

"I'm not mad," Emily reassured her. "You did what you had to do."

The relief on her face was a poem. Tepper smiled. Her shoulders relaxed, along with her body. She debriefed Emily on everything. Complimented her work. It was above and beyond. Tepper would be clearing her false backstory, and reinstating Emily's honorable discharge from the United States Army. She was even going to make sure she got out from under Brasse's thumb.

"You did it, Emily. And I'm going to make sure to fully and unequivocally restore your name."

"That doesn't mean anything to me anymore."

"What do you mean your name no longer means anything to you?" Tepper asked.

"Exactly that. I'd prefer to keep working undercover. My past won't define me, so who says I need one? I'll go wherever you tell me. Do whatever I can to serve my country. I only ask that my father's identity is never revealed, at least not to the media. My mom doesn't deserve that."

"Of course," Tepper said. "Granted."

The thought of Mom finding out who she had married and what he had become was enough to burn Emily's throat with vomit. She had mourned her husband and was disappointed in her daughter. The truth would only make things worse than they already were.

"I want to work," Emily said.

"Then I'll have your next assignment soon." Tepper left with a salute.

A few minutes later Simone finally opened her eyes and looked over. "Emily …"

We are who we spend time with. It's better to be alone than in bad company.

She squeezed Simone's hand and offered her a sincere smile. "I'm here. You're not alone."

Finally, Emily had found the kind of company worth keeping.

What to read next...

John Treadwell is a successful author with a wife and two daughters that he loves. Then he drunkenly hooks up with one of his biggest fans. He's sure he can hide it from his family. After all, the woman lives in London. He can pretend it never happened.

But his biggest fan has bigger plans…

Pick up your copy of Secrets We Keep Today.

A Quick Favor...

If you enjoyed this book, please take a moment to write a short review on your favorite online bookstore so other readers can enjoy it, too.

Thanks so much!

About the Author

Nolon King writes fast-paced psychological thrillers set in the glitzy world of entertainment's power players with a bold, insightful voice. He's not afraid to explore the darker side of human nature through stories featuring families torn apart by secrets and lies.

Nolon loves to write about big questions and moral quandaries. How far would you go to cover up an honest mistake? Would you destroy your career to protect your family? How much of your soul would you sell to get the life of your dreams? Would you cheat on your husband to keep your children safe? Would you give in to a stalker's demands to save your marriage?

Lightning Source UK Ltd.
Milton Keynes UK
UKHW040723060323
418105UK00002B/391